The Crystal Ball

A Rebecca Mystery

by Jacqueline Dembar Greene

americangirl.com/service

To Matthew and Ken, my first fans

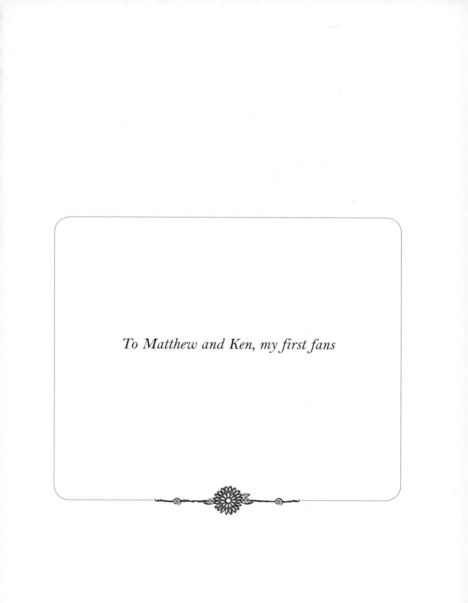

Beforever™

The adventurous characters you'll meet in
the BeForever books will spark your curiosity
about the past, inspire you to find your voice
in the present, and excite you about your future.
You'll make friends with these girls as you share
their fun and their challenges. Like you, they are
bright and brave, imaginative and energetic,
creative and kind. Just as you are, they are
discovering what really matters: Helping others.
Being a true friend. Protecting the earth.
Standing up for what's right. Read their stories,
explore their worlds, join their adventures.
Your friendship with them will BeForever.

TABLE *of* CONTENTS

chapter 1

Times Square Fair

REBECCA CRANKED UP the blue awning
outside Papa's shoe store until only the scalloped
edge framed the top of the window. She was in a
hurry to help Papa close the store early today. Crowds
of shoppers bustled along Rivington Street, and boys
chased one another around the peddlers' carts in a
playful game of tag.

One young boy kept to himself, leaning against
a nearby storefront and eyeing the shoe store. He had
been loitering around ever since Rebecca swept the
sidewalk earlier. Rebecca guessed he was not much
older than her younger brother, Benny. She smiled at
him, but he ignored her and pulled his soft cap lower
over his eyes.

"So many customers buying shoes," said the

pickle seller as he stood beside his cart. "What a busy Friday for your papa. And going home early, yet!"

Rebecca blurted out the afternoon's plans. "We're going to see Houdini do an escape act!" she exclaimed. "It's a free performance right in Times Square."

The peddler arched his bushy gray eyebrows with interest. "Ah, the famous Mr. Weiss," he said, nodding wisely.

Rebecca was perplexed. "No, it's Harry Houdini," she corrected him. "Is Mr. Weiss an escape artist, too?"

"This name you don't know, eh?" commented the peddler. "Believe me, this Houdini fellow is really Ehrich Weiss. His family comes from my neighborhood in Budapest. I read in the papers that in America, his papa was a rabbi." The peddler took a pair of wooden tongs and pushed fat green pickles around in one of the barrels of brine. "But why he changes his name? Is it so hard to say Weiss?"

"Lots of people change their names when they come to America, but I'll bet Houdini is a stage name," Rebecca said. "When I become an actress, I'm going to be Beckie Ruby."

"Hmph!" sniffed the pickle man.

Rebecca couldn't wait to pass on such an interesting bit of gossip to her family. Wouldn't they be surprised to know that Harry Houdini was Jewish, and that he had changed his name?

She opened the door of the shoe store and leaned in. "All set, Papa!"

Papa pushed his billfold into his pants pocket and closed the door firmly. Just as he turned the key in the lock, the boy who had been slouching nearby hurried toward them. Rebecca hoped he wasn't planning to come into the store now. A new customer might keep Papa from locking up. They'd never get home early!

The boy wore shabby high-top canvas shoes. A ragged hole in his left shoe revealed his sockless toe, and a broken shoelace flopped around his ankle. Perhaps, thought Rebecca, the boy had heard that Papa often gave children repaired shoes when their families couldn't afford new ones.

"Sorry, young man, but we're closed," Papa apologized. "Come back tomorrow."

The boy sidled away. Papa put the key into the lock, and then hesitated.

"He sure needs new shoes," Papa said with concern. "I'm sure I could find something—an old pair that would fit him. Maybe I should call him back."

"But Papa, we'll be late for the show. I'm sure he'll come back tomorrow." She was relieved when Papa nodded and dropped the key into his pocket.

Rebecca took Papa's hand and set a lively pace as they walked home. They crossed the broad streets carefully, avoiding rattling horse carriages and sputtering new motorcars. People carried their baskets and bulging shopping bags, and stopped under store awnings to find some shade in the hot afternoon.

Between knots of shoppers, Rebecca thought she
saw the boy with the ragged shoes close behind. She
glanced back. It *was* him, but he turned away, looking
in a shop window.

"Papa," Rebecca said, "I think that boy is following us."

"Maybe he wants to come along and see Houdini
with us," Papa said with a chuckle. He pulled his
watch from his vest pocket and checked the time.
"I hope the rest of the family is ready," he said. "It's
a long way to Times Square."

When they reached their row house, Rebecca ran
up the front stoop and into the entry hall.

Benny had been keeping a watchful eye from the
second-floor landing and gave a whoop. "Yippee!
Papa's home!" he shouted. "Let's go!"

"Hold the horses!" Grandpa puffed, taking
Bubbie's arm as they came slowly down the stairway.
"Such a fuss for this Houdini."

On the landing, Rebecca's older brother, Victor

nudged cousin Josef, who was dressed in work clothes and holding his toolbox. "Come with us," Victor said.

Josef shook his head. "Since the Pomerantzes have gone to Times Square too, it's a good time for me to work on their cabinet. An empty apartment means no complaints about the banging hammer." Josef headed upstairs.

"Don't be late for *Shabbos* dinner," Mama called to him as she followed Grandpa and Bubbie down the stairs.

"From this young man, everyone can learn a lesson," Grandpa declared. "Day and night he works, and every nickel he saves."

Rebecca was glad cousin Josef had moved in with her family for the summer, and she hoped he would stay longer. He was quiet, but he was always interesting when he was in the mood to talk. He had told Rebecca and Benny lots of stories about life in Russia before he came to America. Everything there sounded so different, and also a bit frightening.

Rebecca's older twin sisters, Sadie and Sophie, joined the family as it assembled on the sidewalk. Just then, Mr. Rossi, the janitor, stepped out of his basement apartment holding a broom.

"We're going to Times Square to see Harry Houdini," Rebecca told him. "Why don't you come with us?"

"Thousands of people will be there," Sadie said. "Some of my friends saw Houdini perform in the square last summer. And before the show started, they saw magicians doing tricks right on the side-walk!" She lowered her voice and added, "There were fortune-tellers strolling around, too. Maybe we'll see some!"

The janitor leaned on his broom with a faraway look in his eyes. "In my village in Italy, there were a few women who had the gift of seeing into the future. Not everyone believed, but my family trusted them." Mr. Rossi started sweeping the steps. "Fortune-tellers or not," he said, "I'm gonna stay right here."

"We'll be back before dinner," Mama said. "Why don't you join us tonight?"

"*Grazie* for the invitation," Mr. Rossi said. "You come and get me when you're ready."

Papa took one last look at his pocket watch. "We'd better hurry, or the show will be over before we arrive." He pulled a dollar from his billfold and declared, "This family is taking the trolley."

"Yippee!" Benny exclaimed. "The trolley!"

Rebecca and Benny skipped ahead to the trolley stop. After the family piled on, Rebecca settled into a seat and placed a firm arm around her younger brother. As the trolley pulled away, she glanced out the window and noticed a boy standing alone with his hands in his pockets. Was that the same one who had approached her and Papa at the shoe store? The same one who had followed them as they walked home?

Rebecca pointed him out. "Do you know that boy

from school?" she asked Benny. Her brother turned to look, but it was too late. The car lurched forward and the trolley bell clanged. The bumpy ride was a treat, and Rebecca's thoughts turned to the adventure ahead.

At Times Square, the festive atmosphere reminded Rebecca of the gay crowds that thronged Coney Island. The family bunched together, trying not to become separated.

"Look, Benny! Magic tricks!" Victor exclaimed.

They joined a circle of onlookers surrounding a magician in a shiny satin top hat, white gloves, and a flowing cape lined with red silk. Silently, he raised his arms in welcome and then swept his hat off and gave it a shake. He ran his hand around the inside to show that it was empty. Rebecca could see for herself that there was nothing inside. Then, with a flourish, the magician reached into the hat and pulled out a gray dove. Benny and Rebecca gasped in surprise as the bird flapped its wings and flew off.

The magician bowed as the crowd applauded. Before the audience moved away, he held out the hat for coins. Papa dropped in a few pennies, and the family strolled on.

"I guess he doesn't want that hat to stay empty for long!" Victor said with a laugh.

"You hold your future in the palm of your hand!" cried a woman in a faded purple shawl. "Every line shows your fate."

Rebecca took Sophie's hand in hers and pretended to read her palm. "I see into your future," she droned. "You're going to see a famous escape artist do something amazing! And it's going to happen *very soon*." Sophie rolled her eyes and pulled her hand away as Sadie laughed.

Another street vendor dangled a pole hung with sparkling crystals. The sun caught the many-faceted edges and cast a rainbow of colors. "See the future and bring good luck," he called. "Everything will become crystal clear!"

Rebecca was enthralled by the dazzling crystals. She fingered some pennies in her pocket, wondering if she could afford to buy one. After all, everyone could use a bit of good luck, and even if it didn't work, she could hang the crystal in her bedroom window and watch the colors dance across the walls.

Before Rebecca could ask, Sadie held out a nickel. "Just right," exclaimed the vendor as he scooped the coin from her hand. Sadie chose a long, cut-glass crystal and held it up to the light. "May good fortune be with you always," said the vendor.

"It's beautiful," said Sophie, admiring her sister's purchase.

Rebecca watched longingly as Sadie tucked the crystal into her pocket. "I have some pennies saved up, too," she said, fishing in her pocket.

Bubbie clucked her tongue. "Let's not waste any more pennies on *tchotchkes.*"

Rebecca dropped her coins back into her pocket. It wasn't fair! Sadie had bought a crystal. Why couldn't she? She was about to protest when a stooped woman dressed in a sweeping skirt and flowing scarves stopped two young women nearby. Her gray hair hung in wispy strands, and huge hooped earrings dangled from her pierced ears.

"One dime," she urged. "Just one thin dime and my sewing needle will predict your future."

The two young women hesitated, holding tightly to their purses.

"Wouldn't you like to know about that beau of yours?" the woman wheedled. One of the girls blushed.

"How did she know that girl had a beau?" Sophie marveled under her breath.

"It's quite simple," Mama said matter-of-factly. "She spied two pretty working girls and guessed that at least one of them would have a suitor!"

Sadie and Sophie were as riveted as Rebecca,

staring as the woman pulled a threaded sewing needle from her sleeve. She held it aloft by the end of the knotted thread and let the needle swing freely. "For you," she said, "just five cents and the needle will tell all."

One of the young women glanced sheepishly at her companion and then slowly fished a nickel from her bag and dropped it into the old woman's open palm.

The fortune-teller held the young woman's gloved hand open and suspended the dangling needle over it. "Ask your heart's desire, dearie," she invited.

"Will I be married this year?" the girl asked, color rising in her cheeks. The needle began to swing in a circle as if powered by some outside force. Rebecca watched, mesmerized, as the fortune-teller announced that the answer was yes.

The young woman beamed. She became bolder. "How many children will I have?"

The shrewd fortune-teller thrust out her hand.

"Coins give the needle its power," she cackled. The young woman reluctantly offered another five cents. Again, the fortune-teller suspended the swinging needle over her outstretched hand. The needle pointed straight down and then moved back and forth before slowing to a stop.

"One son," pronounced the fortune-teller with a toothy grin. In a moment, the needle swung sideways once again. "A second son," she crowed. The needle began to make a wide circle. "A daughter!" The needle moved again and again until the fortune-teller had predicted that the young woman would have two sons and five daughters. The two friends linked arms and walked off, their excited whispers trailing in the air.

"Who's next?" cried the fortune-teller. She eyed Sadie and Sophie. "Find out if twins have the same futures!"

Sophie turned to Mama and begged, "Can we try it—*please*?"

Mama quickly nudged the twins away, making little *tsking* sounds as she did so. "I think Sadie has already wasted enough money on that crystal," she said. The twins pouted with disappointment.

"How can someone see the future?" Rebecca asked.

"No one knows the future until they live it," Papa said.

"But then it would be the past," Sophie argued. "That wouldn't help at all."

"Exactly," said Papa.

The family moved along with the surging crowd and soon spotted a small knot of onlookers gathered around a dark-eyed woman. Thick black lashes framed her eyes like fringes of lace, and a shimmery green headscarf contrasted with long black hair that hung over her shoulders in cascading waves. Rebecca stared at a crystal ball the woman balanced in her outstretched hand.

"My crystal, it never lies," the fortune-teller

intoned in a singsong voice. "One dime opens its secrets to my gaze."

A stocky man in rough work clothes and heavy boots stepped from the crowd and handed the woman ten cents. "I try it," he said.

The fortune-teller glanced around warily before snatching the coin and then squinted at the crystal ball. She slowly waved her long, tapered fingers around the crystal as if summoning an unseen power. Rebecca thought the crystal seemed to glow in her hand.

"You have made a long-a journey," the woman said. Her accent sounded similar to Mr. Rossi's, Rebecca noticed. Maybe the fortune-teller was Italian, too. "But you are alone here, no?"

The man nodded solemnly. Rebecca wondered whether the woman meant that the man was alone in Times Square or that he was alone in America.

"Soon you will be joined by someone close to you," the woman predicted.

The man smiled broadly. "I am hoping this. Will be soon?"

The fortune-teller bent her head close to the crystal ball and peered into its depths. "I see smooth travels," she said, and the man nodded fervently. "Soon," she smiled. "Will be very soon." Then she buried the crystal in a pocket in her flowing skirt, the bulge hidden by folds of fabric.

"Grazie," the man said in Italian. Rebecca knew that meant "thank you." It was one of the Italian words she had learned from Mr. Rossi.

The fortune-teller's eyelashes fluttered. "*Prego*," she responded. "You're welcome." Quickly, she drew some papers from a cloth bag that dangled from her arm. She handed one to the man, and he folded it into his pocket. The woman pushed another paper at Mama.

Mama shooed her away, but Rebecca grabbed the paper and stared at the fancy script. "It's a flyer," she said. "'Madame Verona—Knows All, Sees All,'"

she read aloud. Rebecca peered at the bottom of the
advertisement. "She does readings on—" But before
Rebecca could read the address, Mama swept the flyer
from her hands and crumpled it into a tight ball.

chapter 2

Houdini Bound

"MAMA, I WANTED to read about Madame
Verona!" Rebecca complained.

"Never you mind, young lady," Papa said
sternly. "It's against the law in New York to read
the future, or even to advertise such things. If a
policeman sees her telling fortunes, he'll haul her
right to jail."

*So that's why the woman had checked the crowd
before taking the handyman's dime, and probably why
she hid the crystal in a pocket after her reading*, thought
Rebecca. *She was watching out for the police!* "Why is
it a crime?" Rebecca asked. "It seems so harmless.
Besides, maybe it works!"

Papa shook his head. "Some of these people
probably believe in what they do, but plenty of

them are swindlers, convincing people to pay for made-up advice."

Rebecca thought about the fortune-teller's predictions. It would have been easy to guess that the man had come from another country, since he had an accent. Because he was by himself, the crystal reader could say that he was alone and be right. Still, she had predicted that someone was coming to join the man very soon. How could she know that? Then again, she didn't say who was arriving, or where the person was coming from. Was she just making a guess, or did she really see visions of the future in her crystal ball?

"I wanna see Houdini!" Benny piped up, interrupting Rebecca's thoughts. She stood on tiptoe to look over the crowd toward a wooden platform draped in colorful bunting. A few men bustled about the stage, checking heavy wooden stocks attached to a pulley. Others stood at the foot of the makeshift stage, keeping onlookers at a distance.

"The show should start soon," Papa said, patting Benny on the head. "Let's try to get a better view." He angled his way through the crowd and stepped up onto a nearby stoop. Rebecca, Sadie, and Sophie perched on the top step.

"What about me?" Benny asked. "I can't see!"

With an exaggerated grunt, Victor lifted Benny and set him atop his shoulders. "Whew!" he huffed. "You're getting too big to be lifted." Benny beamed from his new vantage point.

Just then, a barker stepped onto the stage. He had a long curling black mustache and wore a bowler hat. A bright red carnation stood out on his lapel. He raised his arms for silence, and a hush fell over the noisy crowd. "Ladies and gentlemen, children of all ages, you are about to see a human marvel." The barker swept his eyes over the audience, and people seemed to hold their breath. "The man you are about to see has cheated death many times over. He has been chained, buried, and submerged and has always found his way free—against all odds! This afternoon, right before your eyes, the one and only Great Houdini will be strapped into a straitjacket and hoisted high above you. Will he escape once again? Or will today be the day that death catches him?"

The barker waved a police officer onto the stage. "Please welcome Captain James Woodward of our illustrious New York City police force. If anyone knows how to bind a man so that he can't escape, it's one of New York's finest!" The crowd let out a roar of approval. "But the Great Houdini won't just extricate himself from his bonds," the barker continued. "He will do it while dangling upside down in midair!" The barker gestured with a great flourish to the side of the stage. "Ladies and gentlemen—the Great Houdini!"

The crowd whooped and whistled. Rebecca stretched as tall as she could, straining to see. How surprised she was when a rather short man stepped

onto the stage. Despite the sweltering heat, he wore
a dapper collared shirt and long trousers. Muscles
bulged beneath his clothes, and his neck was thick
and powerful. Despite his short stature, Houdini
had an impressive air about him, and he radiated
cocky confidence. He bowed deeply, his arms spread
wide, and the crowd went wild, applauding boister-
ously. Rebecca joined the cheers. "Hoo-dee-nee!
Hoo-dee-nee!"

"Tell us what you've got here, Captain," said
the barker.

The policeman held up a strange white jacket
with long, trailing sleeves. A series of leather buckles
and straps bobbed and clacked. "Once a person is
strapped into this straitjacket, there is no possible
way to escape," he explained.

Houdini stepped forward, and the captain
slipped the fearsome-looking contraption onto his
outstretched arms. People in the audience craned
their necks as the officer wrapped the long sleeves

around Houdini's back. His arms were held tightly across his chest, encased in heavy cloth, and the leather buckles were fastened behind his back.

"How can he get out?" Benny wailed. "He's stuck!"

Papa laughed. "That's why we're watching him," he said. "We want to see if he can do it. Won't it be amazing if he does?"

"And now, ladies and gentlemen," the barker continued, "to assure you that Mr. Houdini is indeed strapped in tightly, a hearty volunteer from the audience will make extra sure there is no easy escape. You, sir!" The barker pointed at a man at the front of the crowd. "Would you be so kind as to inspect these bindings?"

The man pulled himself onto the raised platform and stood awkwardly in front of Houdini.

"Good afternoon, my good fellow," Houdini greeted him in a booming voice. "Please forgive me for not shaking your hand." The crowd roared with laughter.

The man made a great show of pulling and tugging at the heavy cloth and the buckles. "Tight as a tick," he declared. "No one could get out of these."

"No one who isn't Houdini, that is," crowed the barker.

Rebecca watched intently as two burly men helped Houdini sit at the edge of the stage with his legs dangling. They clamped his feet into wooden stocks. The pulley creaked as it tightened, slowly hoisting Houdini high into the air. He held his body as stiff and still as a pillar until the pulley came to a halt.

The crowd fell silent. Time seemed to stop as Houdini remained motionless. Rebecca held her breath. She felt a shiver in spite of the warm air. She crossed her arms over her chest and hugged herself.

Papa took out his pocket watch and timed the minutes as they passed. Rebecca could hear the second hand marching forward in her head—*tick, tick, tick*. How long could Houdini survive hanging upside down?

Onlookers began to shift from one foot to another. Someone coughed nervously. Maybe Houdini couldn't escape this time. He was still tightly bound in the straitjacket, and his feet were trapped in the stocks. Why was it taking so long?

Suddenly, Houdini began to squirm and thrash in the air. He sent his body swinging over the heads of the gaping crowd like a giant pendulum. *Tick, tick, tick.*

Sadie and Sophie each gripped one of Rebecca's hands, and the sisters stood staring as Houdini struggled to escape the straitjacket that bound him. Benny buried his face in Victor's hair and then stole a fearful peek at the stage.

Just as the crowd grew uneasy, Houdini whipped his arms above his head, sending the long canvas sleeves flapping like beating wings. He then executed several moves so swiftly that Rebecca could barely see what he had done. With an exultant cry, Houdini pulled the straitjacket over his head and dropped it to the ground in a heap. He thrust his arms wide like a mighty bird in a final flourish above the gaping crowd.

A deafening shout rose from the audience. As Houdini twisted in the air, the burly assistants lowered the pulley and released the escape artist from the stocks. Houdini raised his arms victoriously, basking in the applause, and then bounded from the stage.

"More! More! More!" chanted the crowd. Benny jiggled up and down on Victor's shoulders, whooping with excitement. The barker held up his hands for silence.

"Tonight, at the spectacular Winter Garden rooftop, the Great Houdini will perform a far more dangerous feat. He will be bound in chains and sealed in a water-filled tank. Can he escape that watery chamber? Could anyone survive such a feat? Head to the box office now and buy your ticket. Don't miss out!"

The performance was over. The crowd slowly dispersed, people moving off in different directions. Victor lowered Benny to the sidewalk and rubbed his shoulders. "Start growing taller, Benny," he said. "Your piggyback days are over."

"Did you know that Houdini also taught himself to escape from tied ropes?" Sadie said, her eyes glittering with excitement. "I'll bet I could learn that trick." She lifted her chin with a superior air.

"Don't go thinking you're such a big fish until you do it," Rebecca declared. "In fact, I'll bet I can learn to get out of ropes before you."

"Ha!" Sadie answered. "You could never figure that out."

"Not only will I learn it first," Rebecca said, rising to the challenge, "but I know something about Houdini you don't know."

Sadie scowled. "Fiddlesticks! You don't know anything."

Rebecca savored the attention as everyone in the family looked at her expectantly. "Ah, but I do," she said with a mysterious smile. "And I just might keep it a secret."

chapter 3

Magical Lights

THE TROLLEYS WERE packed as the crowd made its way home. Rebecca's family waited while two full cars passed by until one stopped with almost enough empty seats. Victor and Papa stood and held on to an overhead bar, shifting their feet to keep their balance when the car lurched forward.

Just across the aisle, Rebecca spotted her neighbors, the Pomerantzes. "Hello," she greeted them. "Wasn't Houdini amazing?"

Mrs. Pomerantz's bulky body took up nearly the entire trolley bench. Her thin husband was squeezed against the window. Perspiration dotted her forehead, and she fanned herself with a folded flyer. "If only the Great Houdini could break this hot weather," she said. "Now that would be a magical trick!"

"Papa," Benny asked, "does Houdini use magic?"

"There's no magic," Papa replied, "but it takes real skill and years of practice to master such a feat."

Rebecca thought of the palm reader and the crystal ball gazer she had seen that day. "Fortune-tellers probably have to practice, too," she mused. "But they might guess some of what they predict. I could do that if I noticed every detail about some-one first." She paused. "But I guess that wouldn't really be telling the future, would it?"

Grandpa leaned forward in his seat and spoke up over the clattering trolley. "Back in Russia, there was a woman in our village who told about the future. And she was usually right."

"This woman was no fortune-teller," Bubbie corrected him. "What a *yente* she was." She turned to Mama. "How do you call this in English—a busy-body?" Mama nodded and smiled.

"Well, she made us a match," Grandpa said. "At least she was right when she predicted that we would have a happy life together." He winked at Bubbie.

The girls walked with the Pomerantzes when they all left the trolley near East 7th Street. The sun was low in the sky, and the air was cooling, too.

"I *adore* your brooch," Sadie said to Mrs. Pomerantz, admiring her colorful lacquered pin, which had tiny painted flowers on it.

Mrs. Pomerantz fingered the oval brooch on her dress. "This belonged to my dear mother. She wore it every Shabbos and every holiday."

"These pins are so hard to find here," said her husband. "Lucky you were able to bring this one with you from Russia."

With delight, Rebecca pointed to her own brooch. It had a picture of a leaping hare. "Look, Mrs. Pomerantz, I have a Russian pin, too."

Mrs. Pomerantz smiled. "And yours has a clever folktale behind it. Mine reminds me of our garden back in Russia."

Sadie poked Rebecca's arm. "I always loved that pin, too," she muttered enviously.

Rebecca was crestfallen. "I'm sorry," she said. Her delight in the hand-painted pin fell away. "I didn't ask for it—Bubbie just gave it to me."

"It doesn't matter," Sadie said. "Someday I'll have one of my own." She eyed Rebecca shrewdly and lowered her voice. "Tell you what—I'll make a *real* bet with you. If I learn to escape from a tied rope first, you owe me the pin."

Rebecca was startled. If she made a bet like that and lost, she would lose Bubbie's pin. She swallowed hard. "What if *you* lose?" she asked.

Sadie didn't hesitate. She pulled the crystal from her pocket and dangled it in front of Rebecca. "If I lose, I'll give you my crystal," she said, "and then you can practice telling fortunes."

The crystal glinted in the evening light. Rebecca truly did want the crystal. If she won the bet, she would have the brooch *and* the crystal. She wavered for just a moment and then made up her mind. "It's a bet," she agreed, "and I'm going to win."

When they arrived at their row house, Mrs. Pomerantz turned to the twins. "Again my back is hurting," she complained. "Monday is washing day, but it's not so easy to put the heavy wet clothes on the line. Up and down, up and down, from the basket to the line, such trouble. Maybe one of you girls wants to earn a nickel and hang the wash? I will go to see the doctor."

"I'll be glad to do it," Sadie piped up. "I'll be there first thing."

"Such nice girls," Mrs. Pomerantz said. "We're lucky to have you for our neighbors." The Pomerantzes headed inside. "Good Shabbos," they called.

The Rubins waved from the sidewalk while Papa knocked on Mr. Rossi's door. The janitor came out dressed in a black suit with a white shirt and a tie.

"You sure missed an astounding show," Papa

said, "but we'll tell you all about it over dinner."

Mr. Rossi seemed a bit downcast, but he smiled wanly. "Is nice to share your Sabbath meal," he said. "You are very kind to me."

"It's our pleasure," Mama said, taking Mr. Rossi's arm. "I hope you don't mind chicken and noodles, but I had to prepare everything before we left this afternoon."

Mr. Rossi patted Mama's arm. "When you cook, is always wonderful," he said, "and better than anything I make in my kitchen!"

Josef greeted them at the door and then stood aside to let them file into the apartment. His hair was slicked back, and he was freshly shaven. He smiled shyly, fiddling with his tie, when Mama noticed that the dinner was already heated up. "Josef, you shouldn't have!" Mama exclaimed. "That was so thoughtful."

"I was hungry," Josef said with a soft laugh. "This way we eat sooner!"

The family lined up at the sink to wash, and then
Bubbie ushered everyone into the parlor. The table
was already set with Mama's white tablecloth, linen
napkins, the family's best dishes, and two pairs of
candlesticks holding tapered white candles. Sadie
and Sophie stood before one pair made of gleaming
silver, and Rebecca prepared to light candles in a second pair made of twisted cobalt-blue glass.

Rebecca felt a special glow whenever she lit the
Sabbath candles in her own candlesticks. She beamed
at Mr. Rossi, who had given them to her. She knew
they had once belonged to his wife. The candlesticks
reminded Rebecca of the time when she and the janitor had become friends.

Now Rebecca and her sisters lit the white candles
and together recited the Hebrew blessing to welcome
the Sabbath.

"This makes me remember my Bianca," Mr. Rossi
confided to Rebecca when the prayer was over. "She
always lit candles at special times."

Benny held a ceremonial glass of wine aloft, and Victor guided him through the blessing. Then Bubbie uncovered two braided loaves of hallah bread, and the family recited a third blessing. Mr. Rossi chimed in at the end with a soft "Amen." He looked at Papa. "The Hebrew words I don't know. But a prayer is a prayer, and 'amen' I know!"

Rebecca helped Bubbie serve bowls of steaming broth thick with chunks of chicken, sliced carrots, and soft noodles. Mama sliced the hallah and passed around a straw basket piled with the golden bread.

Victor excitedly told Josef and Mr. Rossi about Houdini's astonishing feat. Sadie and Sophie talked about the fortune-tellers who had mingled artfully with the crowd.

Sophie turned to Rebecca. "So what's your secret about Houdini?" she coaxed.

"If you have one," Sadie challenged her.

Rebecca smiled coyly and slowly ate another

spoonful of noodles. "Well," she said after a long pause, "if you really want to know."

"If we didn't, we wouldn't be asking," Sophie said, rolling her eyes.

"I *heard*," Rebecca said, drawing out her words, "that Houdini's real name is Ehrich Weiss—and his father was a rabbi!" The twins were speechless.

"*Oy*, his poor papa," Bubbie sighed. "He must be turning in his grave. Instead of his son following his footsteps, he becomes a circus act!" She shook her head.

"Maybe his father would be proud of how successful Houdini has become," Victor suggested.

Josef frowned. "Sometimes fathers are never satisfied," he mumbled, almost to himself. Rebecca felt a stab of sympathy for her cousin. She knew he must be thinking of his own father.

Papa gave Josef a pat on the back. "Your father just wants the best opportunities for you," he said.

Rebecca knew that Josef and Uncle Jacob had

been at odds ever since Josef dropped out of school. Rebecca had heard her uncle complaining. "America offers a free education," he would say, "and this boy turns it down!"

Josef tensed. "My father is only going to be happy if I finish high school," he said to Papa. "He doesn't want his son to be a carpenter like him. But I'm too old to be in school. I want to build my own carpentry business."

Rebecca recalled that a few months ago, Aunt Fannie had told Mama that Josef and his father argued whenever they were in the same room. Mama had suggested that Josef move in with Rebecca's family for a while, and Aunt Fannie had agreed that it seemed like a good solution. Now Josef was trying to prove that his plan would succeed.

Sadie changed the subject. "Did you ever have your fortune told, Mr. Rossi?" she asked.

Mr. Rossi nodded gravely. "A woman in my

village could see the future. She gave advice, so people not have problems in their lives. My parents visited her often, and me, I went a few times, too."

Rebecca's eyes widened as Sadie pulled out the crystal she had bought and held it up to the candle-light. The facets caught the light and sent arcs of color sparkling around the room. Rebecca reached out to touch the brilliant crystal, but Sadie dangled it out of reach.

"You'd better concentrate on the rope trick first," Sadie whispered with a sly grin.

Rebecca stole a guilty look at Bubbie. What would her grandmother say if she knew that Rebecca had bet the Russian brooch for Sadie's crystal? But she was too proud to call off the bet. She would just have to learn the rope trick before her sister!

When Rebecca went to sleep that night, her dreams were filled with mysterious fortune-tellers draped in colorful, swirling scarves. She squirmed in her sleep until a creaking sound awoke her. Her eyes fluttered open, and she saw a faint light flickering in her room. A chill raced up her back as she watched dark shadows moving on the wall.

chapter 4

A Handful of Predictions

PROPPING HERSELF UP with one elbow on her pillow, Rebecca peered from the protection of her bedcovers and saw a small candle glimmering on the windowsill. Sadie and Sophie were sitting up in their bed, and Sadie held a swinging sewing needle over Sophie's open palm. When the twins saw Rebecca watching them, Sadie put a finger to her lips. "Shhh," she cautioned.

Rebecca tiptoed across the cool floor, and Sophie pulled back the covers, inviting her to snuggle in. Rebecca was riveted by the swinging needle. "We're telling our fortunes," Sophie breathed. Her eyes sparkled in the candlelight. "Guess what we learned already—I'm going to have six children!"

Rebecca held out her own hand. "Can you tell my fortune?" she asked softly.

Sadie steadied the needle over Rebecca's hand. "Ask a question," she said, "and it swings in a circle if the answer is yes and goes back and forth in a line if the answer is no."

Rebecca closed her eyes and considered a moment. Then she gazed hopefully at the needle. "Will I learn to escape from a tied rope before Sadie?" she asked. The twins stifled giggles and watched as the needle swung left to right. *No.*

Rebecca felt a quiver in the pit of her stomach. Maybe Sadie had controlled the thread to get the answer she wanted. Or maybe she didn't know the proper way to do the needle trick at all. Rebecca hesitated and then held her hand open again. "This is a really important question," she whispered. "Will I become a moving picture actress?" She stared at the needle, willing it to tell her what she wanted to hear.

The needle went wild, swinging in wide arcs and moving left, right, and around. The sisters all stared in surprise.

"What does it mean?" Rebecca asked.

"I think it means even the needle doesn't know," Sadie said.

"Phooey!" Rebecca breathed. "I don't think it knows anything!"

Rebecca crawled back into her own bed, wondering if Papa was right. Maybe the future had to happen before anyone knew what it would be. Or was there really a fortune-teller who could see a person's life unfold in a crystal ball?

"Go ahead," Sadie said to Rebecca over breakfast the next morning. "Tie my wrists together, and I'll get free." She pushed a coiled rope across the table.

"No fair," Rebecca complained. "I haven't had

a chance to practice even once." She took the rope and wound it around Sadie's wrists several times before knotting it tightly.

Josef watched with mild curiosity but didn't wait to see whether Sadie could free herself. He gulped down his tea, took a breakfast roll from the plate on the table, and headed for the door.

"Sit, sit," Mama coaxed. "You need a good breakfast."

"This is plenty, *Tante*," Josef said, using the Yiddish word for "aunt." "I must get back to Mrs. Pomerantz and her cabinet. She hates the noise from the hammering, and she is going to synagogue this morning, so I will bang the nails while she is gone. When she gets back, I'll go to Mr. Adler and start building his bookshelves. I think he won't complain so much about the noise." He took a bite of the roll, pulled on his cap, and left.

Mama watched Josef leave. "No matter how much that boy works," she mused, "it never seems to be enough. He just keeps taking on more jobs and working harder."

"I think he's trying to make Uncle Jacob proud of him," Rebecca said. Mama nodded as she removed plates from the table.

Rebecca finished her breakfast while Sadie struggled with the rope that bound her hands. She pulled her wrists apart and then pushed them tightly together, but the ropes didn't loosen. Rebecca pretended not to be paying attention, but she stealthily watched her sister's every move.

"I give up—for now!" Sadie said at last.

Rebecca untied the rope and dropped it onto the table. "I still have a chance to beat you." But Rebecca's confidence wavered, and she couldn't help remembering the needle's prediction. She stepped quickly into the hallway and scooted up the stairs before Mama could give her a chore.

On the rooftop, Rebecca ducked into a hidden corner behind a pile of wooden pallets. She had created the secret space earlier that summer so that she could read without interruption or simply get away from her noisy family for a while. Now she needed the quiet place to think of a plan.

I just have to concentrate—and practice, she decided. *After all, it's just a trick. It's not magic.* She stepped from her corner, searching for a scrap of rope among the discarded pallets. She kicked at a ripped baseball someone had left behind. That wouldn't help.

She searched the rooftop until she spotted a length of rope peeking out from a stack of lumber near Josef's tools. As Rebecca pulled out the rope, a bone-handled pocketknife clattered from between the boards. The carved handle bore the image of a ship in full sail. *Josef wouldn't want to lose this fancy pocketknife,* Rebecca thought. She placed it carefully in his toolbox and stuffed the rope into her pocket.

"You up here so early?"

Surprised, Rebecca turned to see Mr. Rossi behind her. He ambled to the pigeon cages, holding a pail of water and a bucket of birdseed. He was neatly dressed in his black Sunday church suit and a bowler hat, his tie slightly askew. She smiled at the janitor.

"I'll feed the birds," she offered. "You wouldn't want to get your suit dirty." Mr. Rossi willingly handed Rebecca the pails. She stroked the birds gently after she filled their dishes, and they cooed contentedly. "Are you going to church today?" she asked Mr. Rossi. "It's only Saturday."

The janitor shook his head. "Gotta go to see my brother Aldo in New Jersey," he said. "Talk him out of making a big-a mistake." He seemed distracted as his eyes searched the sky.

"Is something wrong?" Rebecca asked.

"I'm a-worry," he said. "You know Gigi, my favorite blue-gray pigeon?" Rebecca nodded. She knew each of the homing pigeons well, and she knew that Mr. Rossi and his brother used the birds to keep in touch with each other. Each bird could carry a message, flying back to its own roost. "Aldo should-a sent me a message with that bird, but it hasn't come home. Is three days already since I sent a note to my brother. Maybe little Gigi meet with some bad luck, like a hungry hawk." His shoulders slumped.

"I know what you mean about bad luck," Rebecca said. "I was up here playing with my rubber ball the other day, and it bounced right off the roof. I looked all around the alleys between the buildings, but I never did find it." She thought about Sadie's crystal. "I think I need a good luck charm."

"So, even you got a little bad luck," Mr. Rossi said dejectedly. "Not only I lose Gigi, but something else important—the key to my trunk."

Rebecca had seen Mr. Rossi's large leather trunk in the dusty coal cellar and wondered what the janitor kept there. "What's in that trunk, Mr. Rossi?" she asked.

"Is things from long ago," he said. "Now the key

is gone and all those memories is locked away forever." He sighed.

"Your luck will get better," Rebecca said. "Maybe
the pigeon is flying back right now—and the key
will turn up, too." She tried to think of a way to
cheer Mr. Rossi. "Say, I've got an idea. Why don't
I read your fortune? I saw a crystal gazer doing that
yesterday, and it didn't look so hard."

"Do you think you have the gift of second sight?"
he asked. "Maybe you see where is the lost pigeon."

Rebecca hadn't expected Mr. Rossi to take her
offer so seriously. "Oh, no," she said, "I'm just pretending—but I could try." If only she could win the
bet with Sadie, maybe she could really learn to read
the future in the crystal.

Mr. Rossi shrugged. "You try," he said. "You never
know."

Rebecca retrieved the old baseball she had seen
earlier. Holding it in the palm of her hand, she imi-
tated the fortune-teller she had seen in Times Square.

She waved a hand over the tattered ball and pretended to peer into its stringy depths. In a dramatic, gravelly voice, she croaked, "I see you will live to a ripe old age."

"So far, you're right," Mr. Rossi said with an amused smile. "Already I'm ripe!"

Rebecca giggled. "I see a bird flying to you from a great distance," she said and saw Mr. Rossi perk up. "And I predict a long journey ahead for you, too."

Mr. Rossi's eyes widened. "How you know this?" he asked, leaning toward her.

Rebecca wavered. Didn't he realize that she was just talking about things she already knew? She tossed the ball into a corner and returned to her normal voice. "Aren't you going to New Jersey to visit your brother?"

Mr. Rossi's eyebrows knitted together in a deep frown. "Yes, but Aldo is the one taking a long journey," he explained. "Our sister Filomena lives alone in our old home in Italy, and she is sick. Aldo says someone gotta be with her, so he and his wife is going back to the village."

"Oh, Mr. Rossi," Rebecca cried. "I'm so sorry." Now Rebecca understood why the janitor had seemed downcast lately. His brother was the only close family he had in America.

"I tell him is good to want to help Filomena, but with the war in Europe, is not safe to be on a ship. But Aldo is so worried, he won't listen. The big brother always thinks he is right." He shook his head. "Well, I must hurry to catch the ferry."

Rebecca was sorry for the predictions she had made up. Instead of cheering up the janitor, she had made him worry even more.

chapter 5
Things Could Be Worse

REBECCA HANDED BACK the pails and
followed Mr. Rossi down the stairs. Inside her apartment, she stepped around the jacks Benny had tossed
across the kitchen floor. "Watch where you throw
those," she chided him. "You're always leaving them
where someone might trip."

Mama was peeling onions over the sink and
handed Rebecca a short knife. "Just step right over
here and give me a hand," she said, "and you won't
have to worry about jacks."

Rebecca tied on an apron, washed her hands,
and started peeling the papery skins. The fumes
stung her eyes and made them water. She didn't even
bother to ask why the twins hadn't helped. As usual,
they had gone to the library and gotten away with

not doing their share of chores. *Sadie is probably looking for a book on rope escapes,* Rebecca fretted.

Suddenly, she heard a man shout outside. *That sounds like Papa,* she thought. She wiped her streaming eyes with her apron and darted to the parlor window.

On the sidewalk below, a nimble boy lunged at Papa, grabbing at the pocket where he kept his billfold. Papa swatted at the pickpocket, but the boy grabbed the edge of the billfold and pulled.

"A pickpocket is after Papa's billfold!" Rebecca cried. Mama hurried to the window, and she and Rebecca watched Mr. Rossi rush over and pull the boy away from Papa. The pickpocket gave Mr. Rossi a shove and ran off. The janitor's arms flailed as he lost his balance. He fell in a heap and lay still on the sidewalk, as bystanders crowded around.

Rebecca raced down the stairs. Running down the front stoop, she stepped on something that rolled under her foot. She stumbled and fell, scraping her knees and ripping her white stockings. Why, it was one of Benny's jacks! *What rotten luck,* she thought as she pulled herself up and hurried toward Papa.

Mr. Rossi groaned feebly as he lay sprawled on the sidewalk. Papa seemed dazed and patted the billfold in his pocket. The boy had almost gotten away with his bold attack, Rebecca realized, but thanks to Mr. Rossi, he had left without his prize.

A slender man in overalls and a brimmed cap held the gawking crowd back. He kneeled down beside Mr. Rossi. "Don't move too quickly now, old fellow," he said in a reassuring voice. "I'm going to get you home."

"Are you hurt?" Mama called down from the parlor window. Rebecca heard a note of concern in her voice.

"I'm fine," Papa reassured her, "and we're taking care of Mr. Rossi. He's going to be all right."

Rebecca saw Benny's face at the window for a

brief moment before Mama shooed him away and disappeared into the apartment.

"Oh, my hand," moaned Mr. Rossi.

"It might be broken," the man said, examining Mr. Rossi's left wrist and fingers. He turned to Papa. "Can you fetch a doctor?"

Papa nodded. "My daughter will show you where Mr. Rossi lives," Papa responded. "I'll be back as quickly as I can."

"Oh, the poor old man," said a striking woman draped in a sparkling green scarf. Rebecca was captivated by the shimmery threads that laced through it. She was sure she had seen one like it recently, but couldn't recall where. The woman batted her dark eyelashes at the stranger as he helped Mr. Rossi to his feet. "Thank-a goodness you stop to help," she gushed. "Such a hero you are!" Rebecca tried to study the woman more closely, but she melted back into the crowd.

Rebecca led the stranger and Mr. Rossi to the

janitor's apartment next to the front stoop. The kind man helped Mr. Rossi ease onto his couch and pulled an afghan over him. *"Molte grazie,"* Mr. Rossi murmured weakly.

"That's Italian," Rebecca piped up. "It means 'thank you very much.'"

"You're more than welcome," the man said. "I'm glad I was in the neighborhood. Now, just rest until the doctor arrives."

The events that had just occurred seemed as dramatic as a movie scene, but Rebecca knew this was only too real. Perhaps, though, there would be a happy ending after all, Rebecca thought. The kind stranger almost made up for the mean people in the world, like the nasty pickpocket who had tried to steal Papa's billfold.

"I should introduce myself," the man said to Mr. Rossi. "Don Silver's the name, and I'm a handyman by trade."

Mr. Silver's overalls looked brand-new, Rebecca

noticed, whereas her cousin Josef's overalls were worn and frayed and usually flecked with sawdust. Of course, today was Saturday, so Mr. Silver probably wasn't working.

The janitor extended a shaky right hand. "Leonardo Rossi," he said. Then he motioned toward Rebecca. "This my little friend, Rebecca Rubin."

Rebecca smiled at Mr. Silver. He sat close to Mr. Rossi, speaking soothingly and glancing around the tiny apartment.

When Papa returned with the doctor, Rebecca tried to become invisible so that she could stay. Her stockings were shredded, and her skinned knees stung, but she kept silent. If she complained, Papa would surely send her back upstairs. She watched while the doctor checked Mr. Rossi. The janitor's face was ashen, and his hand had begun to swell.

"Two broken fingers," the doctor announced. "But the wrist is just sprained. I'll set those fingers in splints and wrap up the wrist." When the doctor had finished, he tied Mr. Rossi's arm in a clean white canvas sling and gave firm instructions. "You must rest," he advised, "and keep the bandages on until I check you again next week. Do you have a job?"

"He's the janitor for the building," Papa explained.

The doctor spoke firmly to Mr. Rossi. "No work at all before I see how you're healing."

"I'll bring him to your office," Papa promised. He discreetly paid the doctor as he showed him to the door.

His good deed hadn't escaped Mr. Silver's notice. He clapped Papa on the back. "Good man. By the way, did you get a close look at the pickpocket?"

"It all happened so fast," said Papa. "I never saw him coming until it was too late. And he ran off so fast, I only saw his back."

The handyman turned to Mr. Rossi. "How about you? Do you think you could describe the little ruffian to the police?"

Mr. Rossi closed his eyes. "No police," he said.

"Is just a little kid. He pushed me away and I lost my balance. Who knows what he looks like? All-a these kids look the same."

Mr. Silver paced back and forth in the small room. "What a nasty bit of bad luck," he commented.

Was the stranger right about bad luck? Certainly, she and Mr. Rossi were not having very good luck lately. She looked from Mr. Rossi's bandages to her raw, skinned knees. The ripped stockings were tinged with blood. She fingered the metal jack that Benny had left behind. She would give him a sharp scolding!

Mr. Rossi let out a faint murmur of pain, and Rebecca put her hand on his shoulder. "When something bad happens," she said softly, "Bubbie says, 'Things could always be worse,' and it's really true. You're lucky that you weren't hurt any more seriously. And you saved Papa from the pickpocket."

Mr. Rossi's eyes fluttered heavily as if he could barely keep them open. "Lotsa bad luck these days," he said glumly. "Now I miss the ferry, things is even worse. How am I gonna make Aldo understand that he can't go to Italy? Is too dangerous. And if I can't work, how I'm gonna pay the doctor?"

"That's all taken care of," Papa said lightly. "It's the least I could do to thank you for your help. My billfold held yesterday's receipts from the shoe store. If that boy had gotten it, I would have lost more than a doctor's fee."

Mama knocked lightly at the open door and came in holding a plate of *rugalach* pastries. Mr. Silver stood and removed his hat, and introductions were made all around.

As Mama and Papa conferred, Mr. Silver picked up an ornate picture frame standing on a side table and studied it with interest. Curious, Rebecca peered at the photograph. A woman sat stiffly in a cushioned chair wearing an old-fashioned dress, its neckline and hem trimmed in embroidered flowers. A musta-chioed man stood primly beside her, his hand resting lightly on her arm. Next to the couple was a table draped in a lacy cloth, with a pair of candlesticks in the center. *Why, those are my candlesticks!* Rebecca thought, recognizing the familiar twisted glass.

"What a charming picture," said Mr. Silver.

Mr. Rossi looked up. "That's me and my wife, Bianca, on our wedding day back in Italy," he explained. "Those candlesticks was a wedding present from her parents. So long ago."

Mr. Silver smiled. "They must be a family treasure you've kept all these years."

"I've kept them near," Mr. Rossi said. Rebecca felt a surge of pride as Mr. Rossi gave her a wan smile. He moved slightly and winced in pain.

"I'll make some tea," Mama said. Then she noticed Rebecca's bleeding knees. "Oh, dear, Beckie, you're hurt, too?" She frowned. "And look at those stockings—I'll never be able to mend them." But Rebecca was quickly forgotten as Mama busied herself in Mr. Rossi's kitchen looking for a teapot.

Mr. Silver followed right behind her. "Please allow me to help, Mrs. Rubin," he said with a cheerful smile. He peered into cabinets for cups and saucers, searched for a sugar bowl, and opened several drawers until he found spoons. He set out teacups while the tea steeped.

Rebecca heard a rapping at the door and opened it to find Josef. "Is everyone all right?" he asked, out of breath. "Benny just told me what happened."

"Is not so terrible," Mr. Rossi reassured him. "Biggest problem now is how I'm gonna take care of the building." He looked at his bandaged fingers and then at Rebecca. "Maybe your prediction is right. I think maybe is time for me to go home with Aldo, no matter how dangerous."

"But I was just making things up about taking a journey," Rebecca exclaimed. "I didn't mean that you should do it!"

Josef stepped forward. "I can take care of everything until you are better," he declared.

"How can you work more than you do?" Mr. Rossi asked. "All-a the neighborhood want a table, a shelf, a bookcase. You too busy already!"

"It's just until you're well again," Josef protested. "Really, Mr. Rossi, I need the extra work."

Mr. Silver coughed nervously. "Did I mention that I'm a jack-of-all-trades?" he asked. "I'm an all-around handyman, and I just happen to be between jobs right now." No wonder Mr. Silver's overalls were so clean, Rebecca thought. The poor man wasn't working at all. "In fact, that's what brought me to this neighborhood. I was looking for some honest employment," Mr. Silver added.

Mr. Rossi sipped his tea and thought for a moment. "This is better idea, maybe." He nodded to Mr. Silver. "I can't pay much, but I'll give you what I can."

Rebecca saw Josef's shoulders slump, as if all the air had gone out of him.

"Whatever you can spare will be appreciated,"

Mr. Silver said. "I'm glad to help out." He shook hands with Mr. Rossi to seal the agreement. Josef glared at the handyman and then left without another word.

Rebecca tried to fill the strained silence in the room. "I'll take care of the pigeons and the cats," she offered.

Mr. Rossi put down his teacup and patted her arm. "The birds like you because you so gentle. You don't yell and scare them like some kids." He leaned back and closed his eyes, and in a moment he was snoring softly.

They left Mr. Rossi napping on his couch. Just outside the apartment, Mama and Papa paused to thank Mr. Silver for his kindness.

He gestured toward Mr. Rossi's door. "He's going to need a lot of help, and I'm glad to do it. I wouldn't want the building to be neglected while he's recovering. He could lose his job."

Rebecca thought about that as she watched

Mr. Silver heading up the sidewalk, whistling. That surely would be the worst piece of bad luck. Mr. Rossi's apartment was reserved for the building's janitor. If he lost his job, where would he live? Would he have to move back to Italy with his brother? And what would happen to the pigeons?

chapter 6

A Mysterious Message

REBECCA HEARD THE faint chime of church bells ringing after breakfast on Sunday morning. "Poor Mr. Rossi," she said. "I wonder if he's going to miss Mass."

"Perhaps he'll go during the week, when he's feeling stronger," Mama said. She took the dish towel from Rebecca and handed it to Sadie. "You finish drying the dishes, please. Beckie needs to feed the pigeons and the cats." She turned to Rebecca. "Wear your shawl; it's rather cool this morning."

The weather had changed. Dark clouds hung in the air, and Rebecca could hear the wind blowing. Embarrassed that Mama had to remind her of her job, she didn't linger a moment longer but pulled her shawl from the hook and bounded down the stairs to get the food and water from Mr. Rossi.

She stopped in the entryway to drape her shawl around her shoulders and heard a faint rustle in the coal cellar. The basement door in the hallway was open a crack. Rebecca stepped closer and heard a scratching noise. She peered down into the darkness. Was one of Mr. Rossi's cats trapped in the coal bin? It wouldn't be the first time one had gotten stuck. It was easy enough for the cats to jump into the deep bin, but not so easy to leap out.

She hesitated on the first step, her heart beating faster. Rebecca hated the dark basement. Mr. Rossi was the only person who went down there, and that was mostly during the winter to see if more coal was needed for the furnace. Still, Rebecca had promised to look after the cats. She crept down the stairs. She didn't want to frighten the cat and make it hide deeper in the black coal bin.

As her eyes adjusted, Rebecca saw a shadowy figure leaning into the dim light of a hand torch.

A broom was propped against the wall, next to an open trunk. Cobwebs hung from open beams in the musty space. Rebecca took a step closer. Was that Josef? But Josef didn't have one of those newfangled flashlights. Then Rebecca thought she recognized the short, slim figure of Mr. Silver. He held a paper in his hand, close to the glimmering light.

Rebecca cleared her throat. "Is that you, Mr. Silver?"

The dark figure jerked back, fumbling with the flashlight. The paper fluttered to the dusty floor.

"Rebecca?" he asked. "What in the world are you doing down here?"

Rebecca stammered. "I was—well, I—that is, I heard a noise and thought Pasta or one of the other cats was trapped in the coal bin. I didn't mean to startle you."

Mr. Silver let out a nervous chuckle. "I must admit you did give me a scare," he confessed. "It's kind of spooky down here, isn't it?"

Rebecca nodded. "All these spiderwebs give me the creeps. But what are you doing down here?"

"Mr. Rossi told me he lost his trunk key, so I thought I'd see if I could help him with that right away. Actually, opening the trunk was easier than I expected." He held up a large hat pin. "I used this to spring the lock. It worked in a flash. I think Mr. Rossi will be quite pleased to be able to look through his things again." He stuck the pin into the bib of his overalls.

As Mr. Silver steadied the hand torch, Rebecca picked up the paper he had dropped. She brushed off the dust and saw neat handwriting covering the page. "Is this yours?" she asked.

Mr. Silver didn't answer but quickly slipped the paper into a yellowed envelope with an unfamiliar red-tinged stamp pasted in the corner and dropped it into the open trunk. Before he closed the lid, the flashlight beam revealed a neatly folded woman's dress with elaborate embroidery along the neckline.

It reminded Rebecca of the dress Mr. Rossi's wife wore in their wedding photograph. Perhaps it was the very same one, saved all these years.

The letter must be Mr. Rossi's, Rebecca realized. "You really shouldn't read other people's mail," she blurted out. She felt protective of poor Mr. Rossi, injured and alone up in his apartment.

"Read it?" he said, and let out a belly laugh. "I couldn't read that letter if I tried. It was written in some foreign language—probably Italian. I couldn't resist admiring the lovely handwriting, though."

Rebecca relaxed a bit. "I guess it's okay, then," she conceded. Mr. Rossi would certainly be relieved that the trunk was unlocked.

Mr. Silver ushered Rebecca up the stairs, and she breathed more easily as she reached the entryway. "Oh, you forgot your broom," she remarked.

"Yes, so I did," said the handyman. "I'll sweep down there a bit later—starting with those cobwebs!"

Rebecca smiled. "I'll go tell Mr. Rossi that you

got the trunk open. I was on my way to get the bird-seed anyway."

"I wouldn't disturb him now," Mr. Silver advised, placing a restraining hand on Rebecca's shoulder. "He's resting. You wouldn't want to wake him up on account of pigeons."

Rebecca hesitated. The birds needed food and water twice a day. "Well, I guess I can wait a little while," she said. Mr. Silver stood in the hallway, and Rebecca realized she was keeping him from his chores. "I'll come back later." She wandered up to her hidden space on the roof, thinking about Mr. Silver. He was eager to help, but something felt odd about how he had opened the trunk—and one of Mr. Rossi's letters, too.

The next morning, Rebecca plopped down next to Sophie on the front stoop. "Yesterday was so cool, and today feels like summer again," Rebecca said.

In the spaces between the row houses, freshly laundered sheets and clothes billowed in the warm breeze. Monday was wash day in her neighborhood, and today the sun would dry everything quickly. On the sidewalk, Benny tossed a baseball, catching it in his hands. "Isn't Sadie coming out?" he asked.

"I thought she'd be finished hanging Mrs. Pomerantz's laundry by now," Sophie said. "She'll probably be along soon."

Rebecca pulled her jump rope from her pocket. "Maybe I can practice with this before Sadie comes out," she said. "I think she's been secretly working on the rope trick whenever I'm not around." She stared at Sophie. "Tell me—did she find a library book about rope escapes?"

"I can't say anything," Sophie protested. "This bet is between the two of you."

"Phooey!" Rebecca exclaimed. "That means she did!" She handed over her jump rope. "Go ahead and tie my hands. I've got to learn how to get out of a knotted rope before Sadie does."

She held out her hands, and Sophie tied the rope tightly, leaving two long ends dangling down. Rebecca pushed her wrists closer together and then pulled them apart, trying to stretch the rope and loosen the knots as Sadie had. It didn't work at all. "You made it too tight," she fussed. "Not even Houdini could get free!"

Sophie laughed. "If the rope isn't tight, it's not a real escape." She tugged the knots open and handed the jump rope back to Rebecca.

"I guess you're right," Rebecca admitted. "This turned out to be a lot harder than I thought." She felt a lump in her throat, thinking about how easily she might lose her brooch.

"Want to play hopscotch?" Sophie asked, pointing to a hopscotch grid chalked on the sidewalk. She looked around for a couple of smooth stones and handed one to Rebecca. "Come on," she said, pulling

Rebecca from the stoop. "I'm a champ at this!" Sophie tossed her stone and hopped over the square where it landed.

A skinny boy brushed past Benny, causing him to drop his ball. "Watch where you're going!" Benny called after him. He turned to his sisters. "Say, who was that?"

Rebecca glanced over her shoulder. The skinny boy took the steps two at a time and darted into their row house. His jacket bulged, and he held one hand protectively across his chest as if he was holding something underneath.

Rebecca shrugged. "Probably a delivery boy."

"It's too warm for a jacket today," Benny declared, retrieving his ball. "He must be awful hot!"

After Sophie completed her turn, Rebecca tossed her stone, hopped, and reached to pick it up. As she turned to hop back, she saw Mrs. Pomerantz lumbering stiffly toward them, her hand holding on to her hip.

"Did you get the wash hung?" Mrs. Pomerantz asked Sophie, mistaking her for her twin.

Sophie grinned. "It's Sadie who's hanging the laundry. She must be finished by now."

Just then, Sadie stepped outside. She looked surprised to see Mrs. Pomerantz standing there.

"There you are, dear," said Mrs. Pomerantz. She pulled a nickel from her purse and gave it to Sadie.

"I'll take the laundry down after it dries, too," Sadie said, pocketing the coin. She cupped her hand against her forehead to shield her eyes from the bright sun. Without looking directly at her neighbor, she added, "I put the laundry basket under your sink."

"What a sweet girl," Mrs. Pomerantz said. She turned and slowly climbed up the front steps.

When the door had closed behind the woman, Sophie turned to her sister. "It sure took you a long time. Mrs. Pomerantz must have had an awful lot of laundry."

Sadie ignored the comment. "Who's winning at

hopscotch?" she asked instead. "I'll play the winner next." She watched as Sophie and Rebecca continued playing.

Suddenly, the front door flew open, and Rebecca heard an angry voice. Benny and the girls turned to see what the commotion was. Mr. Silver stood in the front hallway scolding the boy in the jacket. "This is a private building, and you have no business being in here."

The boy dashed down the stoop, his jacket flapping open. Curly black hair stuck out from under the visor of his cap.

"And don't let me catch you around here again!" Mr. Silver called to the boy's retreating back. As the boy loped along the sidewalk, something caught Rebecca's eye.

"Did you see his bare toe sticking out of his shoe?" she said to her sisters. "I think he's the same boy who followed Papa and me home from the store on Friday."

"I don't know what he wants around here,"
Mr. Silver said, "but he'll be in a peck of trouble if
I catch him hanging around this building again."
He went back inside and closed the door with a
decisive *thud*.

Rebecca looked at her sisters and shrugged. She
handed over her hopscotch stone to Sadie. "You take
over," she said. "I have to go feed Mr. Rossi's pigeons
and cats." She stepped over to Mr. Rossi's apartment.
The door was open, so she walked inside with a
cheerful "Hello!" Mr. Rossi sat on the couch, his bandaged wrist and fingers cradled on his lap, his hand
badly swollen and purple with bruises. He stared out
the window while Rebecca gathered the supplies.
"I'll take care of everything," she reassured him.

"Sure, sure," Mr. Rossi said absently. "That's-a
good."

As Rebecca carried the pails up the stairs, she
saw Mama and Mrs. Pomerantz on the second-floor
landing talking in agitated whispers. They both

seemed upset. Mrs. Pomerantz's arms waved as she spoke.

Mama shook her head, and Rebecca heard her say, "Nothing like that has ever happened here before. Are you certain you didn't just misplace it?"

Rebecca continued slowly up the stairs with the birdseed and water. She looked down to see Mama and Mrs. Pomerantz still talking, their voices low and their heads close together.

By the time Rebecca reached the rooftop, her head was buzzing with questions. Was Mrs. Pomerantz missing something important? And why was Mama so upset?

Her thoughts were interrupted when a flutter of wings caught her attention. A black pigeon with a ring of cream-colored feathers around each eye flapped in one of Mr. Rossi's cages, pecking frantically at the latch. Rebecca had never seen this pigeon at the roost. Had Mr. Rossi bought a new pigeon to replace Gigi? But surely, the janitor hadn't had the energy to go out or climb up to the roof since he was injured.

"What's the matter, birdie?" she murmured. "Are you hungry?" Then Rebecca saw that the bird carried a message tube affixed to one leg. "Oh! Who put you in here without taking the message?"

Rebecca eased the bird from the cage, fumbling to open the tiny metal tube. The pigeon struggled against her hand, and she held on firmly so that it wouldn't break free. Just as she pulled a thin roll of paper out of the tube, the bird pecked sharply at her finger.

"Ouch!" Rebecca cried, losing her grip. She watched with dismay as the pigeon soared away.

Rebecca gulped. She never should have taken the bird from the cage without permission—and now it was gone. She hurriedly cleaned the birdcages, worrying that she had made a terrible mistake and that Mr. Rossi would be cross with her.

She trudged down the three flights of stairs and

returned to Mr. Rossi's apartment. She put away the pails and handed Mr. Rossi the message. "There was a black pigeon in one of the cages with a note," she said. "Only, when I took out the message, the pigeon flew off! I—I'm so sorry."

Mr. Rossi seemed puzzled. "Gigi came back? And then she flew away again? She wouldn't do that, not after a long, hard flight home—"

"But it wasn't Gigi," Rebecca tried to explain. "Gigi is gray, isn't she? This one was black."

Mr. Rossi shook his head. "I never had a black one."

Rebecca frowned in confusion. Where had the bird come from? "Could the black pigeon be from your brother in New Jersey?" she asked.

"No, no," insisted Mr. Rossi. "That's not how it works with the messages. Aldo keeps a few of my pigeons so he can send messages to me. I keep a few of his. When I am sending a note to Aldo, I put it on one of his birds. See, the birds always go home."

Mr. Rossi looked downcast. "Besides, as soon as my brother makes up his mind to leave for Italy, he gives all his birds away to friends. The only pigeon of mine he still had was Gigi, and she should have been here days ago."

Rebecca was stunned. If the black pigeon wasn't Mr. Rossi's and didn't belong to his brother, how had it gotten into a cage on the roof? She thought about what the janitor had said about his brother. "Didn't *you* want Aldo's pigeons?" Rebecca asked.

"No more birds," he responded. "What I'm gonna do with so many pigeons and no one to send a message to? Maybe I go with Aldo to Italy if I can't make him stay. Otherwise, I'm gonna be all alone here. No family." His voice trailed off.

Rebecca's heart sank. "Please don't move away," she said. Silently, she thought, *I'd miss you.* She helped Mr. Rossi unfold the message, hoping it contained some encouraging news. She watched his expression as he squinted to read the tiny handwriting.

Suddenly, his face turned pale, and the note fell from his hands.

"What is it?" Rebecca cried. She picked up the crinkled paper and tried to read the thin, spidery handwriting, but it wasn't in English. *Mio carissimo leone*, it began. As hard as she tried, Rebecca couldn't make out any more. "What does it say?" she asked.

"Is to 'My dearest *leone*.' This is me."

Rebecca felt more confused. "But I thought your name was Leonardo," she said.

"Is true. But in my country, Leonardo means 'brave like a lion,'" he explained. "My Bianca, she called me her *leone*—her lion." He looked searchingly at Rebecca. "But how can it be for me? No one knows to call me this, not even Aldo. Only my wife, Bianca, and she's gone many years now."

"Then who sent the message?" Rebecca wondered aloud.

"I—I don't know how it can be, but it must be—is from my Bianca," Mr. Rossi stammered.

Goose bumps raced up Rebecca's arms. Surely Mr. Rossi had to be mistaken! Rebecca glanced at the end of the note. There, in thin writing, it was signed, "Bianca."

Rebecca shivered. "But—" It made no sense at all. "What else does the message say?" she asked.

"Bianca says she sees danger ahead, but she doesn't say what." His eyes brimmed, and his voice came through short breaths. "Maybe means I shouldn't go with Aldo. And my brother, maybe he is in danger, too, no?" Mr. Rossi reached for the note again, his hand trembling.

Rebecca started to protest. "But Mr. Rossi, how could your wife—I mean . . ." She couldn't bring herself to say what she was thinking: Bianca couldn't send Mr. Rossi a message if she had died years ago— could she?

chapter 7

Suspicions

REBECCA SAT ALONE on the stoop, knotting and unknotting her jump rope. *If I can see how the knots work,* she thought, *I'll be able to figure out how to get loose before Sadie does.* Somehow, though, her heart was no longer in the competition. How foolish she had been to let her pride run away with her and to make a wager on her precious brooch from Bubbie!

"Good afternoon," came a now-familiar voice. Rebecca set down the jump rope and greeted Mr. Silver.

"What are you up to?" he asked.

"Just trying to stay away from Mama's chores," Rebecca admitted. "I would have gone to help Papa in the shoe store this morning, but he said Tuesdays are very slow."

Mr. Silver held up a small packet wrapped in paper. "I brought a little present from Goldberg's candy shop to cheer up the patient," he said.

Rebecca brightened. "What is it?"

Mr. Silver smiled. "Come with me while I give it to him—maybe he'll share it!"

Rebecca followed Mr. Silver into the basement apartment and watched Mr. Rossi untie the string that fastened the packet. "You're getting much better at doing things one-handed," she remarked.

Mr. Rossi pulled open the paper wrapping. Inside was a cluster of pastel-colored candies. "Sugar almonds is my favorite!" he exclaimed. "How you guess?" He set the packet on the table and gestured to Rebecca and Mr. Silver. "Have some," he offered. Rebecca chose a pink sugar-coated nut and savored the crunchy sweetness. Soon the small mound of sweets had dwindled, and the paper wrapper was nearly empty.

"That's not Mr. Goldberg's regular wrapping

paper," Rebecca noticed. "Whenever I'm in his store, he puts the penny candy in brown paper."

"I guess he ran out," said Mr. Silver.

Rebecca peered at the paper. It looked like an advertising flyer. "Look, it's for a fortune-teller!" she exclaimed, pointing.

Mr. Rossi smoothed out the paper and squinted. "Is not too far from here."

Rebecca read the flyer. *Madame Verona—Knows All, Sees All! Advice—Charms—Predictions.* "We saw Madame Verona with her crystal ball in Times Square!" Rebecca exclaimed. "She told someone's fortune—or at least made some smart guesses."

Mr. Silver slid the remaining candies into a small dish and crumpled up the flyer. "It's pure fakery," he scoffed.

But Mr. Rossi reached for the paper before Mr. Silver could throw it out. "Some people have the gift," he said. "They see omens, good and bad." He glanced at the flyer again. "Maybe Madame Verona sees what danger Bianca's message warns me about."

"Danger?" Mr. Silver repeated. "Why are you in danger?"

"That's the question," said Mr. Rossi, without explaining further. "This fortune-teller might know if I should stay in New York or go back to my village with my brother Aldo. Maybe she tell me if an ocean voyage is safe."

"I guess some people do believe in all that hocus-pocus," Mr. Silver said. "I was told that my grandparents used to consult a fortune-teller back in the old country. They always followed her advice."

"Where you from?" asked Mr. Rossi.

Mr. Silver looked surprised. "Me? Why, I'm from New York!"

Mr. Rossi seemed puzzled. "I mean your family," he said.

"Well, it hardly matters anymore," Mr. Silver said. He rubbed his chin. "Unfortunately, my parents are no longer around, so I try not to think about them too much."

"That's-a sad for you," Mr. Rossi said. "Well, wherever people come from, the older folks like me remember these fortune-tellers." He waved his good hand in Mr. Silver's direction. "You too young to understand the traditional ways." He tucked the flyer into his pocket and addressed Rebecca. "I'm gonna find Madame Verona and ask what the message means, and whether I should go with Aldo." Mr. Rossi pulled himself up slowly. He wobbled dizzily and slumped back down. "Maybe I go tomorrow," he said with a sigh.

"I think you should stay right here and rest," Mr. Silver advised. "You need to get your strength back."

"Maybe," the janitor agreed, "but this is important, too."

Mr. Silver fluffed up a pillow on the couch.

"You so thoughtful," Mr. Rossi said as he leaned

back against the pillow. "Grazie."

"Well, we'll leave you to rest," Mr. Silver said, ushering Rebecca out. He took a broom from a corner. "I'll just sweep the hallways and make sure everything is spiffy." The handyman started with the front stoop, sweeping in wide arcs from side to side.

"You're kind to help Mr. Rossi," said Rebecca.

Mr. Silver smiled. "And *I* think Mr. Rossi is lucky to have a friend like you."

Rebecca ran happily up the stairs. Mama met her at the landing with Benny in tow.

"I've been looking for you, Beckie. Will you take your brother to the park for a while? I can't get dinner ready with him running around my feet."

"I was at Mr. Rossi's," said Rebecca. "He's going to see Madame Verona tomorrow to have his fortune told!" She looked earnestly at Mama. "What do you think Madame Verona can really do?"

"She can pocket his hard-earned money," Mama

replied. "Now pay attention and keep a close eye on your brother."

Benny skipped along beside Rebecca as they made their way to the park. "Josef's in big trouble," he reported. "Mrs. Pomerantz told Mama that her brooch is missing, and she said Josef was the last person in her apartment alone."

Rebecca stood stock-still. *So that's what Mama and Mrs. Pomerantz were whispering about!* "What did Mama say?" she asked.

Benny pulled her along. "Mama said she'll talk to Josef."

Josef would never steal something, Rebecca thought. But how could Josef prove he *hadn't* stolen anything? He often worked alone in different apartments while the tenants were out so that the noise of his work wouldn't disturb them. Then, with a start, Rebecca realized that Josef wasn't the only person alone in the Pomerantzes' apartment—Sadie had been there, too!

Rebecca remembered that her sister had taken a long time hanging out the wash, and then she had gone back into the apartment to leave the basket under the sink. And the other day, coming home from Times Square, Sadie had admired Mrs. Pomerantz's brooch and said she wished she had a Russian lacquer pin. Rebecca's heart beat faster. Could Sadie have taken the brooch? It was hard to imagine, and yet . . .

Rebecca thought of the tiny bedroom she shared with her sisters. There was no place to hide even a small thing like a brooch without Sophie or Rebecca seeing it. And if Sadie had taken it, she wouldn't be able to wear it without being discovered.

As for Josef, he slept on a mattress out on the parlor floor each night. He had no space of his own where he might hide anything. Then Rebecca thought of the roof. Josef could hide something up there with his tools and building supplies. Her mind flashed to the bone-handled knife that had slipped from the stack of lumber. No one would think to look through Josef's toolbox and supplies. She shook the idea away, feeling ashamed of herself for suspecting her own cousin—or her sister!

Down the block, a young man came out of a shop, the door banging shut with a loud rattle. Benny pointed at him. "Look, there's Josef! Let's tell him what Mrs. Pomerantz said." He tugged on Rebecca's hand.

But when they reached the shop, Rebecca froze. Beneath a dingy gray awning, a painted sign on the window read, "Pawnshop—Best Prices for Your Prized Possessions!"

Rebecca felt a sinking in the pit of her stomach. What would Josef be doing at a pawnshop?

"Josef!" Benny yelled. "Wait up!" But the young man had already turned down a side street and was now out of sight.

"*Shah!*" Rebecca said in Yiddish to quiet Benny. "That's not Josef," she said, hoping it was true.

"You made a mistake, Benny."

Her brother started to argue. "Sure it is—"

"No, it's probably just someone who looks a little like him. Now Benny, don't you go telling anyone you saw Josef here, because you probably didn't!" She squeezed Benny's hand. "Promise?"

Benny hesitated. "Okay, okay," he agreed at last, but he didn't seem convinced. "Come on, let's go to the park now!"

While Rebecca sat on a bench watching Benny play, she worried about the stolen pin and Josef's visit to the pawnshop—and pleaded silently for Benny to keep quiet about it. If he let it slip that they had seen Josef there, her cousin might be in serious trouble.

Maybe she could talk to Josef. She didn't want anyone to accuse him of something if there was a perfectly good explanation. But what would she say? She tried to imagine the proper words to ask what he was doing at the pawnshop, but nothing seemed right.

As soon as Rebecca and Benny got back home, they heard a heated discussion coming from the parlor. As Benny settled on the kitchen floor with his ball and jacks, Rebecca crept closer to the parlor. Sadie and Sophie were already eavesdropping near the doorway.

"How do you expect *me* to find them?" Rebecca heard Josef demand. "Do *you* think I took them, too?"

"Of course I don't want to believe that," came Papa's steady voice. "But they might be somewhere in the building. If we could just find them, and return them, I'm sure there would be no questions asked."

Josef tapped his foot on the floor. "That Mrs. Pomerantz," he sputtered. "She said she loved the way I designed her cabinet, but now she refuses to pay for my work. She thinks I'm a thief because I was in the apartment working alone while she was out. But what would I want with her old tchotchke?"

Rebecca slipped closer to the doorway and dared

to peek into the room. Josef's jaw was clenched. "I did leave a few times to get tools from the roof," he said, "but I had a key and I locked the door behind me every time."

"Where were you when Mrs. Pomerantz lost her pin?" Papa asked Josef. "Or this afternoon, when Mr. Adler discovered that his pocket watch was gone? He said that shortly before, you had been in his apartment measuring for new shelves."

Rebecca felt light-headed. Something else had been stolen! She was fairly certain that Josef had indeed paid a visit to the pawnshop. Why wouldn't Josef tell Papa where he had been if he wasn't up to something fishy?

Josef's face turned red. "I know you think I'm guilty. But what about that Don Silver you all like so much? He's in and out of the building all the time. I bump into him everywhere!"

"Try to stay calm," Papa said. "We'll find an answer to this."

"You're just like my father," Josef said angrily. "You think I'll never amount to anything." He rushed from the parlor, brushing against Rebecca as he stormed out of the apartment, his boots clomping on the stairs to the roof.

What would happen to Josef now? Rebecca wondered. Would Papa send him back to Uncle Jacob? Her heart sank. She followed her sisters into their bedroom and closed the door.

Rebecca mulled over Josef's comment about Mr. Silver. She knew that the handyman had quickly made friends with other tenants in the building, and he had offered to repair things for them. He had even cleaned the cobwebs from the basement, just as he'd promised.

The basement! Rebecca recalled the twinge of suspicion she had felt when she saw Mr. Silver looking in the janitor's trunk. Maybe Josef had a point. "What do we really know about Mr. Silver?" she asked her sisters.

Sadie cleared her throat. "And what about that ragamuffin boy who was in our building?" she said. "Maybe he came in and stole things from the empty apartments while Josef was on the roof."

Rebecca had forgotten about the boy. What had he been doing in their building? Maybe he had been prowling through unlocked apartments until Mr. Silver shooed him away. And was he the same boy who had tried to steal Papa's wallet? If so, then he was a likely culprit.

On the other hand, Rebecca reflected, if Sadie had taken the brooch, she might try to point an accusing finger at someone else.

"I don't know who that boy was," Sophie said, "but Mr. Silver is such a nice fellow. We shouldn't jump to conclusions."

The same thing was true about Josef, Rebecca thought. People *were* jumping to conclusions. Was she?

Rebecca stared at Sadie's crystal hanging in

the darkening window. She wished she could
see the future like a fortune-teller, so she would
know what was going to happen to Josef—and
to Mr. Rossi.

chapter 8

A Puzzle in a Pawnshop

AFTER LUNCH THE next day, Mama counted some money into a small purse. "It's Wednesday," she said, "and we need to pick up our meat order from the butcher shop. Will one of you girls do that for me?"

Rebecca reached for the purse. "I'll do it," she offered. She had been hoping for a chance to leave the apartment by herself.

"Wear your shawl, Beckie," Mama ordered. "There's a chill in the air again today."

Rebecca stepped into the crisp afternoon air, grateful that the sticky weather of the past few weeks had finally passed. Gray clouds scudded across the sky. Rebecca hastened along the sidewalk, keeping a tight grip on the purse. When she reached the butcher shop, she walked right past it without stopping. She had something more important in mind.

She headed up the street to the pawnshop. She was hoping to figure out why Josef had been there yesterday, if indeed it had been him.

Rebecca sidled up to the pawnshop and peered into the window. Displayed on a small stand, next to a polished samovar and a set of gold-rimmed china, was a bone-handled pocketknife with a carving of a sailing ship. It looked exactly like the one she had found on the roof. *Of course, Josef has every right to pawn his own knife,* she reminded herself. Then she spotted something more disturbing. Nestled on a piece of velvet was a lacquered Russian brooch painted with gay flowers that looked an awful lot like Mrs. Pomerantz's stolen pin. Beside it was a shiny silver pocket watch. Could it be the one Mr. Adler had reported missing?

Rebecca hesitated before pulling open the shop door, afraid of what she might learn. Cautiously, she stepped inside. A portly man in a striped shirt and a bow tie glanced up from behind a glass counter and eyed her suspiciously. When he noticed the purse, he pasted on a thin smile.

"May I help you find something special?" he asked.

Rebecca wondered how she might get the pawn-broker to give her the information she needed without making him suspicious. Then she remembered how Madame Verona had gotten people to tell more about themselves by making some informed guesses.

She pointed to the window. "The Russian pin might make a lovely present for my grandmother, but I do feel a bit nervous buying someone else's jewelry. Do you think the woman who pawned that brooch plans to come back for it?" she asked, hop-ing the pawnbroker would correct her if a boy had brought it in.

"Not likely," the pawnbroker said, snapping his suspenders with his thumbs. "Things that are left here don't usually go home again."

"Who brought it in?" Rebecca asked nonchalantly, trying a more direct question.

"I never reveal who left what," the pawnbroker said. "People come on hard times, and they like to keep that to themselves. Could be embarrassing, you know?"

"Well, there was a brooch just like that one stolen from my neighbor yesterday," Rebecca said. "It disappeared right from her apartment! I sure wouldn't want to buy a similar one and have my neighbor think I had taken hers!"

"Are you suggesting that I buy stolen goods?" the man said, bristling. "This here's a respectable business. If you want the pin, buy it. If not, get out. I don't have time to waste."

"Well," Rebecca huffed. "I simply cannot take that risk!" She looked impatiently at the pawnbroker, hoping he would offer some tidbit of information. He scowled.

Rebecca was crestfallen. If the pawnbroker wouldn't tell her who had brought in the pin, he certainly wasn't going to tell her about the knife or the pocket watch. Yet how was it possible that all three items had ended up in the window, unless Josef had brought them in yesterday? She left the pawnshop without a word.

She felt certain now that Sadie hadn't pilfered the pin. If she had, she never would have sold it. And surely she had no interest in Mr. Adler's watch. *No*, Rebecca decided, *Sadie would never take something that belonged to someone else. And Sadie wouldn't let Josef take the blame knowing he was innocent.*

But what about Josef? Maybe he had only visited the pawnshop to sell his knife. Then again, the knife had been hidden between pieces of lumber—so perhaps it wasn't rightfully his.

Rebecca hurried back toward the butcher shop, worried that Mama would scold her for dawdling. As the butcher wrapped Mama's order in thick

white paper, Rebecca considered whether to tell
Papa about the items in the pawnshop, and about
Josef's visit there. But she didn't want her cousin
to land in more hot water if there was a reasonable
explanation. The butcher handed her the package,
and she left the shop, lost in thought.

A friendly voice snapped her back to attention.
"Ah, Beckie! You are here!" She looked up to see
Mr. Rossi ambling along the sidewalk. "You are just
the person I wanted to see."

"Mr. Rossi!" Rebecca exclaimed. "What are you
doing here?"

The janitor pointed past the pawnshop to a
brownstone building on the corner of the last block.
"That is where I visited Madame Verona," he said
wearily.

"What was it like to have your fortune read?"
Rebecca asked eagerly.

Mr. Rossi gestured in the air. "Madame Verona
looks into her crystal ball. Deep inside she sees dark

clouds swirling around, and she tells me this means I am troubled. She sees I have received a message warning me of danger." He looked into Rebecca's eyes. "All this she sees in her glass ball! So I show her the message from the black pigeon. She doesn't even open the paper, just-a hold it in her hand." His eyes opened wide in amazement. "Without reading a word, she tells me is from someone close to me— someone who love me very much." Mr. Rossi's voice filled with emotion. "She says the person's name is Bianca!"

"Then what happened?" Rebecca breathed.

"Again Madame Verona looks in the crystal and says the clouds, they are clearing up. She sees a woman in a long dress embroidered with flowers." He touched Rebecca's arm. "This is Bianca, I know! Then Madame Verona tells me the woman is holding two candlesticks—upside down. Black smoke spins around the candlesticks," Mr. Rossi went on, circling his finger in the air. "The fortune-teller says these candlesticks I must bring to her. They will tell what is causing the danger, and what I must do. I gotta bring her your candlesticks tomorrow. I am sorry to ask, *bambina,* but I must borrow them. After Madame Verona tells me what to do, I give-a them back."

Rebecca gasped—*her candlesticks*? "How do you know the ones she saw are the ones you gave me?" she whispered. Something about Mr. Rossi's story gave her an uneasy feeling. Suddenly, she realized what it was: In Times Square, Madame Verona had only talked about the future vaguely, but now she seemed to know every detail about Mr. Rossi's situation. Could she really see such things in her crystal ball? The thought sent a chill down Rebecca's spine.

Mr. Rossi continued to describe the fortune-teller's vision. "Madame Verona says the candlesticks are twisted glass. They are the same ones. The crystal tells clearly—Bianca is sending a message from beyond."

"Oh, I do want to help you," Rebecca said, nearly breathless with astonishment. "But why must Madame Verona *hold* the candlesticks? Why can't she see Bianca's advice in her crystal ball?"

"Madame Verona says if she holds the candlesticks, she will sense the true meaning of this message," the janitor explained. "Bianca maybe is telling me there is danger if I try to go home to my village with Aldo, or maybe there is danger if I stay here. I must find out which choice to make."

Rebecca was torn. What if Mr. Rossi dropped the candlesticks on the way to Madame Verona's? Or—the uneasy feeling pricked at her—what if something else was going on? Was it possible Madame Verona really knew something about Mr. Rossi's future, or was she just a swindler as Mama and Papa had said?

"If I don't bring the candlesticks to Madame Verona," Mr. Rossi said, his eyes pleading, "I won't know if I should stay or go with Aldo."

Rebecca couldn't refuse Mr. Rossi's request, even if she lost the candlesticks forever. "Of course I'll bring them to you," she said softly.

That evening, Rebecca took the delicate candlesticks from her trunk, running her finger lightly over the cool glass. *I have lighted Sabbath candles in these every Friday night since Mr. Rossi gave them to me,* she thought. The candle flames always glinted off the ridges of the blue glass. With a sigh, she wrapped them in a soft linen cloth and placed them gently in a calico bag. Holding them close, she carried them down to Mr. Rossi.

"Grazie, bambina," Mr. Rossi said. "You will have them back before is time to light them again."

chapter 9

A Blind Alley

THE NEXT MORNING, Rebecca was still brooding about the fortune-teller's request. She barely paid attention as she and Sophie cleaned the parlor. Rebecca dusted the furniture, and then her sister rubbed each piece to a shine with beeswax.

"Sadie almost escaped from the rope," Sophie confided. "I tied her hands quite tightly, and she nearly got out."

Rebecca shook the dust cloth out the window. Was Sadie going to beat her, just as the swinging needle had predicted? She felt discouraged but tried not to show it. "What's the trick?" she asked.

"I promised not to tell," Sophie mumbled.

"You can tell me," Rebecca coaxed. "After all, it's not fair if she has a secret trick."

Sophie lowered her voice to a whisper. "You shouldn't have wagered your pin. That crystal is only worth a nickel!" She looked toward the parlor doorway to see if Sadie was watching. Then she stepped into the kitchen and returned with a dry dishcloth. She swiftly pushed it into her sleeve. Once Rebecca had a chance to observe the slight bulge of the cloth, Sophie pulled it out again. "Remember, I didn't tell!"

As Rebecca tried to figure out how hiding a cloth up her sleeve might help her escape from a rope, Mama and Bubbie put on their hats and took their shopping bags. "We're taking Benny with us to buy vegetables," Mama said. "When you girls are done with the furniture, please see if you can get through the mending." She turned toward the bedroom. "Sadie, come and help with the chores," she called. Rebecca frowned at the pile of socks that needed darning and shirts that needed buttons sewn back on.

A cool breeze blew the curtains, and Rebecca turned to close the window. Outside, she spotted Mr. Rossi shuffling along the sidewalk. In his good hand, he carried Rebecca's calico bag. Rebecca caught her breath.

Sadie sauntered into the room. "Are you all right, Beckie?" she asked with a concerned look.

"It's Mr. Rossi," Rebecca said. "I'm worried about him." She explained to the twins what he had told her about Madame Verona the previous afternoon. "How could the fortune-teller have known about the candlesticks unless she has real powers?"

Sadie shook her head. "I think Mr. Rossi is about to be hoodwinked, just as Papa and Mama said."

Rebecca was surprised to hear that Sadie thought the crystal ball reading might be just a trick. After all, her sisters had wanted to have their fortunes told. They had even tried to do it themselves with the swinging needle. But the skeptical looks on the twins' faces made Rebecca even more concerned about Mr. Rossi.

"What can we do?" Rebecca asked. "He's on his way to Madame Verona's right now."

"We need to warn him before it's too late," Sadie declared. "Beckie—we should follow Mr. Rossi. We might even be able to stay with him when he meets Madame Verona."

Rebecca perked up. "Do you think so?"

"You two go ahead and try to help Mr. Rossi," Sophie said. "I'll do as much of the mending as I can, but you'd better get back before Mama does. She wouldn't want you anywhere near the fortune-teller's parlor."

"Come on, Beckie," said Sadie. "Let's try to catch up to Mr. Rossi and convince him to come home."

"What if he won't?" Rebecca asked as they hurried outside. She knew how important Mr. Rossi thought it was to hear Madame Verona's predictions.

"Then we'll have to stick close to him and make

sure he isn't cheated," said Sadie.

Rebecca was grateful to have Sadie's help. Still, she couldn't help wondering if her sister was really just hoping to see how the fortune-teller read the crystal. In fact, now that she thought about it, Rebecca had to admit that she was rather curious herself.

The girls hurried along the sidewalk, but Mr. Rossi had too much of a head start. Rebecca didn't see him anywhere. As they approached Madame Verona's neighborhood, all the tenement buildings looked similar with their tall front stoops and cluttered fire escapes. Boys hung around in small groups or pitched a ball against the steps. Girls chattered together as they watched over their baby brothers and sisters. Traffic and pushcart peddlers filled the street.

Rebecca and Sadie turned a corner and scanned the street in both directions, searching for Mr. Rossi. Farther up the block, Rebecca could see the butcher shop, where Mr. Rossi had pointed out Madame Verona's brownstone, and the pawnshop, where she and Benny had seen Josef.

"There he is!" Sadie cried, pointing across the street. "Mr. Rossi!" she called out, waving frantically. "Wait!"

The girls began to run after him, but clattering wagons clogged the street, blocking their way. At last, they dashed across the busy road. Sadie raced ahead and caught up to Mr. Rossi just as he trudged up the front steps of a brownstone. The bag holding the candlesticks swayed in his hand.

A faint movement at a first-floor window caught Rebecca's eye. She looked up to see a shadowed face peeking between the folds of a heavy drape. Then the curtain flopped closed. Was it Madame Verona, watching for Mr. Rossi's arrival?

"Please don't go in," Rebecca pleaded with him. "We—we think Madame Verona is trying to trick you."

"No one can really see the future," Sadie added with concern.

"I know what is real and what is make-a-believe," Mr. Rossi said gruffly. "Madame Verona, she has the gift. You girls go home now. Go on."

The front door opened, and the fortune-teller appeared in a long dressing gown and layers of gauzy purple scarves. Her hair hung in loose waves, partially covering her face. She glared at the sisters with piercing black eyes. "Come, my friend," she beckoned Mr. Rossi, taking his arm.

"Let us come in with you," Sadie begged him.

"Visitors not allowed," declared Madame Verona. "Too many people, nothing appears in my crystal." She opened the door just enough to let Mr. Rossi in, and then shut it firmly behind her.

Rebecca scrambled up the steps and pulled at the handle, but the door was locked. She gave the door a kick of frustration.

Sadie slumped down on the front stoop of the

brownstone, her chin in her hands. "Now what?" she fretted.

Rebecca looked around. Was there another window where they might get a view into the fortune-teller's parlor? Down the street, the pawn-shop door opened. Rebecca watched—and felt a pang of relief when she saw that the boy who came out was much too short to be Josef. The boy ran up the crowded sidewalk, darting easily between people and baby carriages. He rushed past Rebecca and Sadie. Just before he turned into the alley alongside the brownstone, Rebecca caught a glimpse of something familiar—a broken shoelace flapped against the boy's high-top canvas shoe. She squinted and saw that his bare toe protruded from a hole.

Rebecca gripped Sadie's arm. "That's the boy who followed Papa and me from the shoe store last Friday," she said in a hoarse whisper. "And he's the same one Mr. Silver chased from our building! I'll bet he's the pickpocket who tried to steal Papa's billfold, too. Hey, maybe that's why he was lingering by the shoe store at closing time. I wonder if he was planning to steal Papa's money that night—or maybe a new pair of shoes." Suddenly, Rebecca thought of something. She rushed down the steps and looked toward the alley where the boy had melted into the shadows. "Sadie, what do you suppose he was doing in the pawnshop?"

"How would I know?" Sadie asked.

Rebecca explained how her suspicions about Josef had led her to the discovery of a Russian brooch and a carved-bone pocketknife in the pawnshop that looked identical to Mrs. Pomerantz's missing brooch and the knife she'd seen on the roof. "And there was a silver pocket watch there, too," Rebecca added.

Sadie didn't seem convinced. "If that boy's the thief who took the pin and the pocket watch to the pawnshop, then what was Josef doing there?"

Rebecca tried to puzzle it out. "Well, what if Josef is in cahoots with that boy?"

Sadie bit her lip. "Gosh, Beckie, I hope not."

Rebecca pointed down the alleyway where the boy had gone. "I'm going to follow him and see if I can find out anything. You wait here for Mr. Rossi."

"What if he comes out before you get back?" Sadie asked. "Where should we meet you?"

Rebecca looked down the street, toward the pawnshop. A large maple tree shaded the street corner. "If I don't see you here on Madame Verona's stoop," she said, "I'll meet you by that tree."

Sadie nodded. "Be careful," she warned. "That boy is stronger than he looks. Remember how he pushed Mr. Rossi."

Rebecca stepped cautiously into the shadowy alley and crept alongside the building, covering her nose at the stench of rotting garbage. She tried to search inside a small shed, but the door was firmly padlocked. Reluctantly, she checked the outhouse, but it was empty except for buzzing flies. Soon she reached the end of the alley. Rebecca was baffled. The boy had vanished.

"He couldn't just disappear into thin air," she muttered under her breath. "Even Houdini couldn't do that!"

Then Rebecca heard the faint sound of a creaking door hinge. She ducked behind a mound of trash and peered out. Against the building's stone foundation, a low wooden flap opened, and a small girl stepped out. Dark braids draped over her shoulders from beneath her straw hat. The girl smoothed the long skirt that fell to her feet and hurried toward the street.

What an old-fashioned skirt, Rebecca thought. Perhaps the girl had only recently come to America. Some immigrants wore clothes they had brought from the old country until they got settled.

But Rebecca had more important things to consider. If the trapdoor led into the building, perhaps that's where the boy had gone. *I've got to find out,* she decided. *And maybe I can also discover a way into Madame Verona's parlor.*

She crouched outside the flap, listening for any sound within. Hearing nothing, she eased open the cover and ducked inside.

chapter 10

The Secret Chamber

REBECCA LOWERED THE flap silently and blinked. She was stooping in a dark, stone-lined tunnel laced with gurgling pipes. What had the little girl been doing in there?

She crept deeper into the crawl space and came to a low chamber where she was able to stand. A flashlight hung from a nail on the wall, and Rebecca grabbed it. Before she could turn it on, she was startled by a low cooing that echoed through the small space.

She fumbled with the switch on the hand torch and flicked it on. "H-hello?" she called in a shaky voice. There was no answer. She shined the beam toward the sound and was stunned to see a black pigeon inside a wooden cage. Around its eyes were thin cream-colored rings. It looked just like the bird that had carried the mysterious message to Mr. Rossi. But how could it be the same pigeon? And if it was, how had it ended up down here?

Rebecca flashed the light beam around the room. It played over the rough stone walls, revealing several steps leading around a corner. Cautiously, she climbed the stairs, stepping lightly so that her shoes wouldn't announce her approach.

Rebecca entered a long, narrow room that seemed to run along the length of the building. Faint light filtered through a dirty window, silhouetting a row of hanging scarves, two wooden frames holding wigs, and several packing crates. It seemed to be some sort of storage area. Rebecca aimed the light into every corner in case the boy was waiting to spring out at her, but she was alone.

An emerald-green scarf sparkled with shimmering silver threads and jogged Rebecca's memory. She studied it more closely. Why, Madame Verona had been wearing this scarf when Rebecca saw her in Times Square! She was certain she had seen it somewhere else, too. But where? Rebecca had a fleeting memory of a woman melting into the crowd around Mr. Rossi just after the pickpocket had fled. The woman had worn a green scarf laced with sparkling threads. Rebecca wasn't sure whether there was a connection to all that had happened, but she decided to take the scarf, just in case. It could be an important clue. Since her dress had no pockets, she stuffed the scarf into her sleeve for safekeeping.

Rebecca scanned the walls of the cramped space. Spotting a glimmer of yellow light coming through a small hole in the wall, she stepped up onto a wooden crate and put her eye to the hole. To her great surprise, she found herself looking straight into Madame Verona's parlor.

Mr. Rossi was sitting across from the fortune-teller, who was draped in her shimmery purple scarves. Between them stood a round table covered in black velvet, with a sputtering white candle and a glowing crystal ball in the center. The fortune-teller waved her hands slowly around the crystal, as if caressing the air around it. She leaned in closer. "Ah, yes. I see candlesticks surrounded by swirling black smoke," she intoned. Rebecca was riveted by the woman's silky voice.

Madame Verona fixed her steady gaze on Mr. Rossi. "Did you bring-a them to me?" she asked.

Mr. Rossi rested the calico bag on the table. With his good hand, he struggled to unwrap the cloth that protected the candlesticks.

The fortune-teller's eyes sparkled as she smoothly took the bundle from him. "*Molto bene,*" she said in Italian. "Very good. Now I must hold them and feel the aura." She swiftly removed the candlesticks from the wrapping. Clutching one in each hand, she closed her eyes. Instantly she grimaced and began to chant in a low, raspy voice that seemed to come from deep within her chest: "*Bad luck and danger come to you, from twisted pillars made of blue."*

Rebecca felt a prickle of fear at the ominous words.

Mr. Rossi's face crumpled. "But I have them since my wedding," he protested. "How can-a be bad luck?"

"Fortunes change," Madame Verona murmured. "Have you not had difficult times of late?" She leaned over the crystal, and the deep voice came again. *"I see something important is-a lost. I see you fall on a sidewalk."*

Rebecca was stunned. How could she see all this in her crystal ball? Was it possible that Madame Verona had been the woman wearing the green scarf on the day Papa and Mr. Rossi were attacked? What had she been doing there?

Mr. Rossi nodded weakly. "But these candlesticks not mine now," he explained. "I give-a them to a friend."

"Woe betide the owner of these accursed

candlesticks!" Madame Verona prophesied. She set them on the table as if they were too dangerous to hold for another moment. "There is danger ahead for any in their path."

Rebecca's heart raced. She thought about her problems the past few weeks—her lost ball, her stumble on the jack. And what about all the bad luck in their building—the missing brooch and watch, the pickpocket and Mr. Rossi's fall, Josef's troubles . . . were these strokes of bad luck all caused by the candlesticks? Was such a thing possible?

"What I'm gonna do?" Mr. Rossi asked plaintively.

The fortune-teller beckoned with a long, thin finger, and a child appeared from the shadows of the room. Rebecca stifled a gasp. It was the girl who had come from the hidden chamber in the alley! Although Rebecca had been watching closely, she hadn't seen anyone else in the room. It was as if the child had simply materialized in Madame Verona's parlor.

The girl held out a wooden box and opened the lid, and the fortune-teller placed the candlesticks inside, cushioning them in a velvet cloth. "I will destroy this curse for you," she said. "I bury them deep under the earth and speak a charm that make-a them harmless."

"No, no!" Mr. Rossi protested. "These cannot be cursed—they belonged to my good wife, my Bianca!"

The fortune-teller didn't waver. "Trust the crystal," she said. "When the candlesticks are gone, your fortunes will change. You will travel far without danger and find new happiness."

With the box in her hands, the girl stepped away from the table. As she did so, she tripped slightly over the hem of her long skirt. A high-top canvas shoe was visible in the candlelight—a shoe with a hole revealing a bare toe. Rebecca's heart skipped a beat. Why, it wasn't a girl at all—it was the boy Rebecca had been looking for! He must have donned a wig and girl's clothes from the hidden chamber.

The long, old-fashioned skirt was hiding his knickers and shoes. He hadn't disappeared in the alley—he had ducked into the secret chamber and disguised himself! He had passed right by Rebecca, fooling her completely.

"The crystal never lies," the fortune-teller declared flatly. She closed the lid on the box and extinguished the candle with one breath. The parlor was plunged into darkness, with only a hint of light seeping in around the drawn window curtains. Madame Verona spoke from the shadows. "The crystal knows all and sees all."

Rebecca blinked into the small peephole, trying to make out what was happening. Without warning, a trapdoor slid open next to her head. She pressed flat against the wall, hoping she wouldn't be seen. Gradually, she discerned two small hands placing a box on a narrow shelf set into the wall behind the trapdoor. She froze, afraid to move a muscle, until the door slid closed.

Trembling, Rebecca reached over and grasped the wooden box, startled by its weight. *The candlesticks!* she thought. She couldn't let them be buried in the ground. The things that had happened to her and to Mr. Rossi were simply unfortunate events—weren't they?

Rebecca heard Mr. Rossi in the darkened parlor. "I change my mind," he said. "Give-a them back!"

Rebecca wanted to call through the peephole and let Mr. Rossi know that the candlesticks were safe. But she realized that if she was going to *keep* them safe, she had to escape with the candlesticks before anyone discovered she had them.

Before Rebecca could turn around, a strong hand clamped over her mouth and held her in a tight grip. She let out a muffled cry. A familiar voice whispered in her ear. "Don't make a sound, or you'll regret it." Rebecca didn't have to see the face to know it was Don Silver.

chapter 11
A Knotty Problem

DON SILVER'S HAND tightened over her mouth. "Not a peep!" he hissed. "Is that clear?" Rebecca nodded, and he released his grip and pulled the box from her hands. "I'll take this. These candlesticks are worth a tidy sum, and my pawnbroker will pay handsomely for them." He let out a soft, satisfied laugh.

Rebecca couldn't imagine how he knew about the hidden entrance into the building. It was as if he had come into the storage room to receive the box when the boy passed it through the trapdoor. Rebecca didn't understand how the boy, the fortune-teller, and the handyman might be connected, and yet here was Don Silver, apparently retrieving the candlesticks Madame Verona had taken, with help from the very same boy. Was Don Silver regularly selling things that the fortune-teller swindled from people like Mr. Rossi?

Don Silver set the box down and pulled a thin scarf from the nearby rack. He bound Rebecca's wrists tightly and then knotted another scarf around her ankles. She sank to the floor.

The handyman tested the knots with a tug. "That should hold you for a while." He chuckled and added, "A very long while." He pocketed the flashlight and grabbed the box that held the candlesticks.

Rebecca wondered if Mr. Rossi had already left Madame Verona's building. As soon as Don Silver was gone, Rebecca decided, she would yell as loud as she could.

Then she heard a distant call. "Beckie! Beckie, where are you?" It was Sadie, calling from the alley! Would Sadie find the hidden flap that led inside?

The handyman leaned over Rebecca. "Remember—not one sound or you will regret it."

His threat sent a shiver of dread through her.

Sadie's calls stopped, and Rebecca barely made out her sister's faint voice saying something about "meeting place." Sadie was probably telling Mr. Rossi about the plan to meet at the maple tree. Rebecca wanted to call out to her sister, but with Don Silver standing guard, she didn't dare make a sound.

"I'll let someone know you're down here on my way out of the city," he said, "and not a minute sooner." Rebecca swallowed a lump in her throat and fought back tears. She watched helplessly as Don Silver ducked into the low passageway and slipped out. The wooden flap banged shut with a decisive thud.

Now Rebecca was alone. Her only hope, she realized, was to loosen the knots herself. If only she had mastered Houdini's trick of untying a rope! But Don Silver had pulled the fabric so tightly that there wasn't an inch of wiggle room to loosen the bindings. Rebecca pushed her wrists close together and then pulled them apart as forcefully as she could, hoping to stretch the fabric. The scarf slackened ever so slightly, but not nearly enough to slip her hands out.

The dim light from the small window was fading, and now Rebecca could barely see the knots looped around her wrists and ankles like a tangled maze. She was losing valuable time! Don Silver would be long gone by the time she got out of the chamber—if she ever did.

Oh, why didn't I practice with Sadie, instead of making such a foolish bet? If she and Sadie had shared what they had learned, Rebecca thought, she might already be free.

She slumped back against a wooden crate. So many thoughts swirled in her head. If Don Silver was in cahoots with the young pickpocket, then that would mean that he had deliberately taken advantage of Mr. Rossi's injury to get inside the janitor's apartment. Memories flooded back to her—Don Silver asking about the candlesticks in the wedding picture . . . and then searching through cabinets, supposedly to look for teacups. Of course—he was trying to find the candlesticks! He must have known they were valuable the moment he saw them in the photograph.

Voices filtered again through the thin wall behind Rebecca. Don Silver was inside Madame Verona's parlor! It only made sense that the handyman and the fortune-teller were scheming together, too, Rebecca realized.

Madame Verona and Don Silver were talking in hushed voices. Rebecca strained to hear, but she couldn't understand a word. With a shock, she realized why—they were speaking Italian! Yet the handyman had spoken English without any trace of an accent, and he had assured Rebecca that he couldn't read Mr. Rossi's letter. Clearly, Rebecca realized ruefully, he had lied. And if Don Silver could speak and read in Italian, that meant he could write it, too—which meant that *he* was the one who had planted the message on the black pigeon. He knew Bianca's secret name for Mr. Rossi because he had read it in her letter.

Rebecca pictured the day the pickpocket had come into her building. The weather had been sweltering, yet his jacket had bulged. Why would he wear a jacket on a hot summer day—unless he was hiding something? It must have been the black pigeon—a homing pigeon that would return to Madame Verona's building. Don Silver had made a show of chasing the boy away, but he must have done that only to avoid suspicion. And if the handyman was the thief in the building, then it was he who had sold the stolen items in the pawnshop.

Rebecca felt a bit like Houdini, trying to untangle a complicated knot. But if she was going to save the candlesticks, she had to untie the knots that bound her now. She tugged frantically at the scarf binding her wrists. She should have realized that Madame Verona couldn't possibly have known so

much about Mr. Rossi—unless someone had told
her. And Don Silver had given her all the details she
needed! Rebecca couldn't believe she had been so
completely hoodwinked by the handyman's friendly
manner.

Rebecca heard a flurry of footsteps in the parlor,
then a door slammed shut. She shivered. The stone
floor of the chamber was cold. She wished she had
put the green scarf she had found around her shoulders instead of in her sleeve. Maybe she could pull
it out using her teeth, and then somehow—Rebecca
flashed to an image of Sophie pushing a dishcloth
into her sleeve and then pulling it out. Sophie had
been giving her a hint about the rope escape trick . . .
would it work?

Hoping against hope, Rebecca nudged her chin
against her wrist until she felt one tiny corner of the
silky green scarf sticking out. Grasping it between
her teeth, she pulled, and a few inches edged out.
Again and again she bit onto the scarf and tugged

until at last it was completely free. The green scarf had taken up just a bit of room inside her sleeve. Now that it was removed, the knots Don Silver had tied no longer bound her hands so tightly.

Rebecca pulled hard against her bindings, loosening them a little more with each try. Time seemed to stand still as she rolled the scarf over her legs and eased it slowly over her hands. Suddenly the fabric rolled off and dropped to her lap. She quickly untied the knots that bound her feet and yanked off the scarf. She was free! She scrambled down the steps, ducked through the passageway, and ran out of the alley toward the maple tree where she and Sadie had agreed to meet.

As Rebecca approached, Sadie stepped out from the shade of the maple tree. "Are you all right?" she cried, enveloping Rebecca in her arms. "I've been frantic!"

"Hurry," Rebecca urged. "We've got to get to the pawnshop before Mr. Silver gets away."

"Mr. Silver?" Mr. Rossi asked in confusion. "Where does he go?"

"I'll explain later," Rebecca called over her shoulder. She dashed down the street, dodging between a fruit peddler's cart and another piled with old clothes. Mr. Rossi huffed along behind her, leaning on Sadie's arm.

Rebecca burst into the pawnshop with the others close behind. The startled pawnbroker dropped his pencil onto the glass counter with a clatter. Looking at the group over the rim of his tiny glasses, he recognized Rebecca, and his thin smile returned. He tucked the stubby pencil behind his ear. "So, you're back for the Russian pin, eh?"

Rebecca shook her head. "Has a man been in here to sell a pair of blue candlesticks?" she gasped. "They were just stolen from my friend."

The pawnbroker's face went stony. "I told you before," he said, "I don't deal in stolen goods."

Mr. Rossi was leaning against the counter, trying

to catch his breath. The pawnbroker dragged a tall stool from behind the counter and helped him sit down. Then he turned his attention back to Rebecca. "I think you'd better explain yourself, young lady."

In a tumble of words, Rebecca spilled out what had happened in the past hours. She related how Madame Verona had swindled Mr. Rossi out of his candlesticks; how Don Silver, who had come to get the candlesticks, had caught her spying in the secret chamber and had tied her up; and how he had confided his plan to sell the candlesticks and leave town. "Now we've got to see that he's caught—and get the candlesticks back!"

"I don't want to get messed up with this business," the pawnbroker said. "This is nothing but trouble. I'm calling the police."

As the pawnbroker stepped into a room at the back of his shop, the front door opened again. Rebecca turned, half hoping and half dreading it would be Don Silver coming in. But it wasn't the handyman at all. Rebecca blanched. It was her cousin Josef!

He froze, a guilty look on his face. "Wh-what are you all doing here?" he sputtered.

"The question is, what are *you* doing here?" Rebecca asked.

"What are you talking about?" Josef asked. "I'm here trying to get back something that belongs to my family," he said, giving the pawnbroker a pointed look as he returned to the front counter.

The pawnbroker cringed under Josef's steady gaze. "You're driving me nuts, coming in here every other day," he complained.

"It's your own fault," Josef exclaimed, anger rising in his voice. "I've saved more than enough, but you keep raising the price, you crook!"

Rebecca was puzzled. "What are you trying to buy?" she asked.

Josef looked pained. "I want my mother's ring," he explained softly. "She had to pawn it when Papa and I lost our jobs after the strike at the clothing factory. We needed the money to pay the rent. It broke Mama's heart to lose that ring. She said Papa gave it to her back in Russia before they were married. If I could get it back, maybe my father would finally think I am—" Josef faltered and didn't finish the thought. Instead, after a pause, his voice rose again in agitation. "My father sold that ring for just four dollars, but when I tried to buy it back, *he* said it would cost six dollars." He pointed angrily at the pawnbroker. "Six dollars!"

"Hey, that's business," the pawnbroker said with a shrug of his shoulders. "I have to make a little profit."

"But I did save up six dollars," Josef said. "It took months. When I came back with the money, he said the price was *ten* dollars! I even pawned my pocketknife, and he still wouldn't sell me Mama's ring for a fair price!"

So that's why Josef has been working so hard and saving every penny, Rebecca thought.

"I think the police might want to hear about that ring," Sadie said.

"And that Russian pin and the pocket watch that were stolen from our neighbors," Rebecca chimed in. "The police might be interested in how those ended up here, too, since they have been reported as stolen."

The pawnbroker shifted nervously. He opened his mouth to protest—and then seemed to think better of it. He unlocked a case that stood against the wall and removed a dainty gold ring with a bright red stone embedded in the center. He gritted his teeth and thrust the ring into Josef's hands.

"I'd appreciate it if you'd keep me out of this candlestick business," he said. "In return, I'll sell the ring back to you for the same price I paid—four dollars even." Then he reached into the display window and retrieved Josef's knife, the Russian brooch, and the silver pocket watch. "Take these, too," he said. "I can't risk any problems with the police."

Josef slipped the ring onto his pinky finger

for safekeeping. "What do you call this stone in English?" he asked. "In Russian, it sounds like our name—*rubin*."

Sadie touched the gemstone. "It's called a ruby," she breathed. "Gosh, Josef—your father was so romantic!"

Josef's neck flushed, but his serious expression didn't change as he carefully took the remaining items from the pawnbroker. Then he turned to Rebecca. "Why did *you* think I was coming here?"

Rebecca felt her cheeks redden with shame. "I—I wasn't sure. Benny and I saw you leaving the pawnshop just after things had been stolen from our building. When I went into the shop the next day, Mrs. Pomerantz's pin was there, right next to Mr. Adler's pocket watch—and your knife."

She was filling Josef in on all that had happened with the handyman, the fortune-teller, and the pickpocket, when the door opened and Don Silver strode in, the wooden box tucked under his arm.

He stared at the group in pure astonishment.

"There's Mr. Silver!" Rebecca whispered to the pawnbroker. "He's the thief!"

"Silver?" repeated the pawnbroker. "You're mistaken. This is Dominic Silvestri. He's one of my best customers." He smiled broadly and started to greet Don Silver when Sadie broke in.

"Whatever he calls himself, he's got Mr. Rossi's candlesticks!" She and Rebecca grabbed for the box, but Don Silver stepped deftly aside.

"I have nothing here except a gift," he said, smiling calmly. "This silly girl is completely mistaken."

The pawnbroker reached for the box and set it on the counter. Then he looked sharply at Rebecca and asked, "Can you describe what's inside this box?"

"Two candlesticks, made of twisted blue glass," she stated flatly. "And they belong to Mr. Rossi."

Mr. Rossi rose from the stool. "These come from Italy long ago," he said softly to the pawnbroker. "This man, and Madame Verona, the fortune-teller up the street—they swindled me to get them."

The pawnbroker glanced from Mr. Rossi to Don Silver. "Let's just have a look," he said, opening the lid.

"I can see this isn't a good time," Don Silver said smoothly. "I'll come back tomorrow." He snatched the box, slammed the lid shut, and rushed to the door. But just as he reached for the door handle, Josef blocked his path. They tussled, and Josef was able to keep the handyman off balance. When Don Silver took a swing at Josef, the younger man wrestled him to the floor and pinned him down.

Suddenly, the clanging bells of a police wagon filled the air. Through the display window, Rebecca saw two burly policemen rushing toward the pawnshop.

chapter 12

Fortunes Reversed

BEFORE DINNER THAT evening, Sadie and Rebecca discussed the day's events in their bedroom. Sadie revealed how worried she and Mr. Rossi were when Rebecca didn't come to the maple tree right away, and Rebecca explained all that had happened in the dark chamber and how she had escaped.

"So, you really did beat me at the rope escape after all," Sadie admitted quietly.

"Yes," Rebecca said. "Once Mr. Silver—or Mr. Silvestri—left me in the fortune-teller's chamber, I really had to escape. I worked a lot harder to get out of those knots than I would have if I had been practicing in the kitchen!"

Sadie held out her crystal. "You won, fair and square," she said with a rueful smile. "It's yours."

But Rebecca shook her head. "Let's forget we ever made that bet," she said. "If you just let me use the crystal for fun now and then, you can borrow my pin anytime you want."

There was a knock at the front door, and Rebecca heard voices in the parlor. "It's Mr. Rossi!" She and Sadie joined the family in the parlor.

"Please have a seat, Mr. Rossi," Mama was saying.

Mr. Rossi sat stiffly in a chair, with the wooden box perched in his lap. But Rebecca thought his eyes had a glow she hadn't seen in a while. "Today my little pigeon Gigi comes home, and she carries a message from my brother," he announced. "Is good news. Aldo says Filomena's health is much better. So Aldo and his wife stay in New Jersey. With the war in Europe, finally he agrees is not safe to travel there. Maybe, when the war is over, we make a visit together."

Then his happy expression faded and he became serious. "It was too easy for Mr. Silver to convince me that I needed to go to Madame Verona to end my bad luck and discover whether a trip to Italy would be safe." Mr. Rossi looked sheepish. "He wrapped the almond candies in a flyer for the fortune-teller just so I would see it. Such a fool I was." His cheeks reddened. "I guess I wanted someone else to make a hard decision for me, so I was too willing to believe in the crystal ball. I wonder how many trusting people Madame Verona has fooled by pretending their precious belongings is bringing bad luck!" He patted Rebecca's hand. "If you hadn't helped, I would have lost your candlesticks." He handed her the box.

Rebecca shook her head. "Now that I know how valuable they are, I can't keep them, Mr. Rossi."

The janitor smiled. "You think I didn't know they were valuable? Foolish I may be, but not so dumb." He gestured toward the box. "These were a gift from me to you—and a gift you can't give-a back."

"You mean you still want me to keep them?" Rebecca asked. She glanced at Mama and saw her nod slightly. Rebecca hugged Mr. Rossi. "They will always be my treasure," she said.

Josef sat down on the sofa beside Papa. "I think our entire building was a real treasure trove for Don Silver," he said. "And he was going to let me take the blame for the things he stole! I hope people here will be able to trust me again."

"Don't worry," Papa said. "We returned the stolen items to the neighbors, and they know that you were completely innocent. And—" Papa paused dramatically—"you'll be receiving a letter of commendation from the police for stopping a wanted thief from escaping." He gave Josef an encouraging pat on the shoulder. "When your father hears all you've done, he's going to burst with pride."

"Maybe he'll see that carpentry is the work I love," Josef said hopefully. "I know I can build my own business."

"I'm going to take you around to the shopkeepers on Rivington Street," Papa said. "They all need display shelves and cabinets. You're going to have plenty of work."

Josef beamed, and Mama gave him an approving look. Then she turned to Papa. "I still don't quite understand how Don Silver, Madame Verona, and the pickpocket are connected," she said.

"It was quite a scheme," said Papa. "According to the police, Don Silver often faked a rescue of someone the pickpocket had targeted just to get invited into the person's apartment. Don Silver pretended to be a friend, but he was really looking for things to steal."

"As soon as Mr. Silver saw the candlesticks in the wedding photograph," Rebecca said, "he must have known they were valuable. He wanted to find out whether Mr. Rossi still had them, so he stuck around."

"And when he doesn't find them," Mr. Rossi added, "he finds a way to get me to visit Madame Verona and bring-a the candlesticks to her."

"And once he realized that Josef was working in

different apartments, he probably thought he would see what else he could steal," said Papa.

"But how did he get into those apartments?" Josef asked. "I always locked the doors behind me when I left."

Rebecca thought a moment. "Mr. Silver opened Mr. Rossi's trunk lock with a hat pin. I'll bet he is an expert at opening door locks, too." She turned to Mr. Rossi. "I saw Mr. Silver reading one of your letters when he got your trunk open. He claimed he couldn't read Italian, just so I wouldn't think that he was snooping around!"

Mr. Rossi looked down at his hands. "So that's how he knew Bianca used my special name." His eyes misted. "Always in my heart, I knew the message the black pigeon brings couldn't be from her, but I wanted to believe."

He looked so wistful, Rebecca tried to think of a way to make him smile again. She pulled her shawl over her head and dangled Sadie's crystal close to the light. "Ahh, *Signore* Leonardo," she said in a raspy voice, "I see you have made a long journey—just as I predicted you would, many days ago."

"So you did, bambina," said Mr. Rossi. "But tell me, what journey did I make?"

"You traveled a long and winding path to gain wisdom," Rebecca intoned. "And you didn't have to travel more than a few blocks!"

Inside Rebecca's World

Not many people during Rebecca's time knew
that Harry Houdini, the famous escape artist, was a
Jewish immigrant whose real name was Ehrich Weiss.
His family emigrated from Budapest, Hungary, to
America when Ehrich was four years old. They settled
in Wisconsin.

Young Ehrich took several jobs to help his family
earn money. According to legend, he took a job assist-
ing a locksmith. He quickly learned how to pick the
locks that his mother put on the kitchen cupboards to
hide freshly baked sweets! When he was nine years
old, he joined a local circus as a trapeze performer,
marking the beginning of his onstage career.

When Ehrich was a teenager, his family moved
to New York City. He worked as a necktie cutter at a
factory and met a young man named Jacob Hayman
who also dreamed of being a performer. Together
they began a magic act and called themselves The
Brothers Houdini, after a popular French magician,
Robert-Houdin. After a few years, the pair split up,
but Ehrich continued to perform as Harry Houdini.
Soon he was performing grand public stunts on city
streets, like the dangerous straitjacket escape that
Rebecca's family watched.

Harry Houdini was a household name by the

time Rebecca's family saw him perform in Times Square in 1916. His foreign-sounding name and immigrant background, along with the mystique of his spectacular acts, earned him the respect of many immigrant families, who saw him as a symbol of success.

Houdini used his fame and knowledge to disprove spiritualists' claims that they could communicate with the dead. He believed that it was wrong to prey on grieving people by using phony devices and tricks to make them think they were speaking with the spirits of loved ones. Houdini added lectures and demonstrations of the spiritualists' tricks to his performances onstage and even testified as an expert before Congress when a bill was introduced to ban fortune-telling swindles in Washington, D.C.

Houdini wasn't the only one trying to put a stop to fortune-tellers' practices. In New York City, the police received many complaints from people who had been swindled by fortune-tellers. Some had received bad medical advice from fortune-tellers claiming to have healing powers. Others were immigrants whose superstitions made them easy targets for fortune-tellers' scams. In 1910, the police began to round up fortune-tellers under a new law that forbade anyone but a priest or minister to foretell the future.

GLOSSARY

Italian Words

bambina *(bam-BEE-nah)*—a young girl or baby girl

grazie *(GRAHT-zee-eh)*—thank you

mio carissimo leone *(MEE-oh ka-REE-see-mo lay-OHN-ay)*—my dearest lion

molte grazie *(MOHL-teh GRAHT-zee-eh)*—thank you very much

molto bene *(MOHL-toh BAY-nay)*—very good

prego *(PRAY-go)*—you're welcome

Signore *(see-NYOH-ray)*—Mr.

Yiddish Words

Bubbie *(BUH-bee)*—Grandmother

oy *(OY)*—an expression of dismay or frustration

rugalach *(ROO-gul-ahk)*—a small pastry, often filled with nuts or jam

Shabbos *(SHAH-bohs)*—Sabbath

shah *(SHAH)*—shush, shut up

Tante *(TAHN-tuh)*—Aunt

tchotchke *(CHAHTCH-kuh)*—a trinket or bauble

yente *(YEN-tuh)*—a woman who spreads gossip

Read more of REBECCA'S stories,

available from booksellers and at *americangirl.com*

∽ *Classics* ∾

Rebecca's classic series, now in two volumes:

Volume 1:
The Sound of Applause
Rebecca uses her talents to help cousin Ana escape Russia. Now she must share everything with Ana—even the stage!

Volume 2:
Lights, Camera, Rebecca!
Rebecca gets the best birthday present ever—a role in a real movie. But she can't tell anyone in her family about it.

∽ *Journey in Time* ∾

Travel back in time—and spend a day with Rebecca.

The Glow of the Spotlight
Step inside Rebecca's world and the excitement of New York City in 1914! Bargain with street peddlers, and audition for a Broadway show. Choose your own path through this multiple-ending story.

∽ *Mysteries* ∾

Suspense and sleuthing with Rebecca.

A Growing Suspicion: A Rebecca Mystery
Who is jinxing the Japanese garden where Rebecca and Ana volunteer?

The Crystal Ball: A Rebecca Mystery
A black pigeon carries an eerie message to the coop on Rebecca's rooftop. Only a visit to a fortune-teller will reveal its meaning!

A Sneak Peek at

A Growing Suspicion

A Rebecca Mystery

Step into another suspenseful
adventure with Rebecca!

THE NEXT MORNING, the girls waited just a few minutes on the corner before the Tanakas joined them. As they approached, Rebecca couldn't take her eyes off Mrs. Tanaka. Slender, and barely taller than Rebecca herself, the gardener's wife moved gracefully along the sidewalk in delicately embroidered slippers. Instead of a typical shirtwaist and skirt, she wore a pale lavender *kimono* that reached the tops of her feet. It was tied with a wide purple sash and was lovelier than any costume Rebecca had ever seen. The flowing sleeves on the kimono reminded her of a butterfly's wings.

"She's beautiful," Rebecca whispered to her cousin.

"Please meet my wife," Mr. Tanaka said.

"Glad to meet you," the girls said in unison.

Mrs. Tanaka bowed and murmured, *"Konnichiwa."*

Rebecca guessed that must be the Japanese word for "Pleased to meet you," or perhaps "hello."

It hardly mattered. Mrs. Tanaka was so captivating that Rebecca began to picture her as the star of a movie, with lavish sets and costumes. Ever since she'd had the chance to play a small part in a moving picture with Mama's cousin Max, there was nothing Rebecca loved more than acting.

"Normally, my wife would wear a kimono only on special occasions," Mr. Tanaka explained, "but when she greets visitors at the teahouse, she must reflect the image of a traditional Japanese woman. Each day, she also demonstrates the art of creating flower arrangements called *ikebana*."

The girls nodded. Rebecca couldn't guess what such flowers looked like, but she was sure they must be beautiful.

On the way to the Botanic Garden, the trolley sped along Flatbush Avenue, past spanking-new apartment houses, small shops, and shiny motorcars that sputtered and honked as they passed by. Rebecca barely noticed. Instead, she stole glances at

Mrs. Tanaka. The gardener's wife kept her eyes lowered and didn't say a word.

Maybe she doesn't speak English, Rebecca thought. She knew it had been terribly hard for Ana and her family to learn English when they first arrived. Aunt Fannie and Uncle Jacob still often spoke Yiddish, their own first language. But Rebecca didn't need to have a conversation with Mrs. Tanaka to admire her flowing silken robe and the wooden hair combs that fastened a sleek bun at the back of her pale neck. Mrs. Tanaka was lovelier than any of the real actresses Rebecca had met. She envisioned herself starring in a moving picture, costumed in a flowing kimono just like Mrs. Tanaka's. The movie would be titled *The Gardener's Wife* . . . and naturally the poster advertising it would feature her.

Rebecca was shaken from her fantasy when, after just a few stops, Mr. Tanaka stood abruptly. He escorted his wife and the girls off the streetcar and through the black iron gate of the Brooklyn Botanic

Garden. Immediately, Rebecca felt as if she had entered a magical space. Trees bursting with lime-green buds lined the path, and in every direction she saw low shrubs with purple blossoms and patches of vivid yellow daffodils set off by clusters of bright blue flowers.

It was as if she had been transported from the bustling city into another world. "I thought we were going to see an ordinary flower garden," she said, "but this is like stepping into the Emerald City!"

Ana reached for Rebecca's hand and gave it a soft squeeze. "It really is as dreamy as *The Wonderful Wizard of Oz*," she murmured.

"I think Mr. Tanaka must be the Wizard," Rebecca whispered.

Together, the girls followed the Tanakas along the broad dirt path to a low, white-painted building surrounded by a large unplanted garden plot. A tall woman stood near the front door. She wore a long gray skirt with a thick woolen sweater buttoned over her shirtwaist. Her hair was pinned up in a sweeping pompadour.

"Oh," Ana murmured. "That's Miss Ward, the woman who came to my class."

Miss Ward looked up from her clipboard. "Good morning, Mr. and Mrs. Tanaka. Are you bringing some new gardeners to my workshop?" she asked brightly. "The Children's Garden is almost ready to plant."

"Good morning," said Mr. Tanaka, pressing his hands together and giving a short bow. "My young neighbors love to garden, but they are not yet old enough for your class. Instead, I plan to show them around the Japanese Garden and have them assist me this week."

Miss Ward's expression clouded. "That would be highly irregular. Children shouldn't be in the garden without supervision."

"I will look after them and keep them busy,"

he explained, pushing his glasses up. "They will learn quickly."

Miss Ward stared pointedly at the cousins until Rebecca squirmed. "You certainly could not find a better tutor," she said at last. "Mr. Tanaka has been the backbone of the Japanese Garden area." She gave a soft laugh. "I do believe he can predict when every leaf will sprout and every bud will bloom.

"If you are willing to assume responsibility, Mr. Tanaka, perhaps we can try it out just for today." Then she addressed the girls. "I hope you young ladies will not keep Mr. Tanaka from doing his job. Lately, some unfortunate incidents have added to the work here. Just last week a cluster of irises was torn out near the pond. It was difficult for Mr. Tanaka to save them." Miss Ward shook a finger sternly at the girls. "Although you're not in my workshop, you must follow the same rules as the students. Be sure not to interfere with Mr. or Mrs. Tanaka," she cautioned, "and don't wander off on your own. Stay on the paths at all times, and do not pick so much as a dead weed unless you're told to."

Rebecca swallowed hard. She hadn't expected a gardening teacher to be stricter than her teacher at school!

JACQUELINE DEMBAR GREENE is the author of the American Girl series about Rebecca Rubin. The books have won national awards, as have many of her picture books and historical novels. Ms. Greene has also written nonfiction books and several Rebecca mysteries. Besides writing, Ms. Greene loves to explore ancient areas that still hold secrets, such as the magnificent ruins and burial sites in Egypt and the tumbling pyramids in Mexico, Guatemala, and Honduras. Ms. Greene enjoys gardening, hiking, biking, and photographing the exotic places she visits.